RIBBON OF FIRE

RIBBON OF FIRE

Allan Campbell McLean

CANONGATE · KELPIES

First published 1932 by Collins
First published in Kelpies 1985
Second impression 1989

Copyright © 1962 Allan Campbell McLean

Cover illustration by Jill Downie

Printed in Denmark
by Nørhaven Rotation

ISBN 0 86241 074 6

*The publishers acknowledge the financial assistance
of the Scottish Arts Council in the
publication of this volume*

CANONGATE PUBLISHING LTD
17 JEFFREY STREET, EDINBURGH EH1 1DR

To Margaret MacPherson

Chapter 1

I saw the police long before they clapped eyes on me, and I could have been over the turf dyke and away down any one of a dozen hidden paths – that a stranger would never have set foot on, narrow sheep tracks that clung to the cliff face, twisting and turning through shelving rock and scree and clumps of stunted bush – to the safety of the shore far below, if I had been of a mind to keep clear of them. But I stayed where I was, my back against the green turf dyke, eyes narrowed against the glare of the sun; a sun that had beggared the harvest by his absence but shone fiercely now that October was in, the sparse crops gathered, and the cold, wet summer long since dead and gone. There was no choice for me, anyway; the grazing cattle all around made sure of that. I had to stay with the beasts I was herding, because there were gaps in the dyke where they could plunge to their death, and in our island the loss of a cow is felt near as bad as the loss of one's own. Our cattle are our life. Many's the time I have heard the old men tell of the year of the great famine when the crops failed and the people were that far gone in hunger they had to bleed their beasts for food. That was near forty years ago, back in 1846, but you have only got to be slow in taking potatoes, or grumble at the least thing in the way of food, and they are speaking of the year of the famine as if it was yesterday, telling how they watched their mothers mixing the blood with oatmeal, frying it in slices, and themselves that desperate for a bite they very near ate their fingers when the last crumb had been licked clean from their hands. So you do not need to be a prophet to know that without cattle there would be no life for us in this place.

That is why I stayed where I was watching the advancing policemen. There were six of them marching line abreast across the moor towards me, big men every one of them, their high, pointed helmets giving them the stature of giants. Glasgow police, that was a sure thing. Part of the squad of fifty that Sheriff Ivory had summoned to our island, to help keep the law by his way of it. Well, if they were hoping to seize the men who had cast down the laird's fine new dry-stone wall – a wall enclosing forty acres of our best grazing ground that he had taken for himself with no word of a penny off our rents to make up for the loss – they were going to be disappointed, for there was not a man in the place. Every man in our township had made off, as soon as it was light, on the long trek across the moor to the harbour in the south to welcome Lachlann Ban home from Edinburgh. And the same was true of all the townships for miles around. Every man who was able – and many a one who was not, as my mother had said, with a sniff of disapproval – had gone to greet Lachlann Ban. It would be night before they were back, and, supposing the police waited for them, how could a handful of men in uniform hope to quell hundreds of our own men, not scattered, for once, like chaff in the wind over miles of lonely glen and narrow strips of arable land with a waste of moor between, but grouped around Lachlann Ban, close gathered in strength and courage? Why, the police were not born who would face a gathering like that, with Lachlann Ban at its head, himself new out of Calton Jail and not the man to take kindly to the sight of uniforms in the place.

All that was true enough, but, meantime, I had to face them alone, and I was not fancying it, I can tell you. My heart was fairly thumping and it did not slow down any when the biggest of the policemen, a man with an angry red

8

face and three stripes on his arm, suddenly barked: 'Here, boy!'

I got to my feet as slowly as I dared, resenting being shouted at like a dog, wondering what it was they wanted of me, why six of them should have sought me out, fear knotting my stomach at the thought of all the things I had done against the law. But they were not to know that I had helped my father pull down the first stone from the laird's new wall less than a month ago. That work had been done at night, the new moon our only witness, and every man in the township had been summoned to the task, so that none could be tempted to whisper the name of a neighbour to the factor in the hope of gaining favour with the laird.

But there were other things – the factor's Notice, the one warning that whelks could not be gathered from the shore without the payment of a fee to the laird, and forbidding the lifting of drift timber washed up by the sea. I had torn that notice down from the door of the shop and ripped it in pieces – at night, mind you, but I had been foolish enough to speak about it later. Aye, and there was many a thing besides. I quaked at the thought of them all.

'Are you deaf, boy?' the sergeant roared. 'Get a move on!'

I stumbled towards him, knowing fine that if it had been Lachlann Ban he had bellowed at the same one would not have moved a muscle.

He looked down at me as he might have looked at a craven dog that had been slow to answer his bidding for fear of a blow, and he stuck his thumbs in the broad leather belt and swelled his chest, and said: 'Follow me.' And with that he turned on his heel and strode off the way he had come.

Two of the other policemen had moved behind me as if they thought I was about to take to my heels. Good grief, that was not my idea at all; it was as much as I could do to stand secure on my legs, far less run for it. One of them pushed me forward. I twisted round to protest that I must stay with the cattle but a hand seized the collar of my jersey and forced me on. I tried to wriggle free and got a stunning blow on the head for my pains. After that, I went quietly, half-choking with the jersey pulled tight about my neck. The sergeant never looked round once, striding out across the moor in the direction of the new school, its tall chimney stack lifting over the rising moor like a pointing finger.

Three of the policemen were ahead of me; the other two behind. One of the three said, 'I am telling you, the general is not pleased. They say he is wanting the marines brought in.'

I knew fine who he meant by the general – General Kemball-Denison, the laird. Not that I had ever clapped eyes on him, for he had other estates on the mainland and was hardly ever in the place. But his name was on all the factor's notices, although there were some who said that the factor did many a thing in his name that the general had no word of.

'Naw, naw.' Another policeman shook his head. 'Not the general. The sheriff more like. The sheriff is the one to sort them.'

The third one glanced round. I heard him say softly: 'Well, I wouldn't fancy being in yon fellow's boots whatever the rights of it.'

A quick understanding of the English is not easy come by when your natural tongue is the Gaelic. You hear the words right enough, but you have to change them in your mind into the familiar Gaelic before their meaning becomes clear. And I was without boots, walking barefoot, which helped to deceive me. We had almost reached the school before I realized that by 'yon fellow' the policeman had meant me.

There was a wagonette drawn up outside the gates of the school; a beauty of a coach alongside, four jet-black Highland ponies between the shafts, the sun gleaming on their silken backs and polished harness. The scholars must have been dismissed from school for a crowd of them stood gaping at the coach, drifting away every time the coachman lifted his whip to them, and surging forward again, like the silent rush of an incoming tide, the moment his back was turned. I caught a glimpse of my sister Mairi, her eyes fairly popping. She looked that pale and scared, the sight of her gave me courage, if you can believe such a thing.

I called: 'Away and herd the cattle, Mairi,' and the fellow who had a grip on my jersey gave me a shake and pushed me on through the gates and up the steps to the school, so I had no chance to see if she obeyed.

Mr Nicolson, the *Maighstir*,* was standing at the door, looking that solemn you would have thought he was there to witness my execution. My heart gave a leap at the sight of him, much as a prisoner in olden times, cast down among his enemies, must have been uplifted by the sight of a familiar tartan, knowing that aid was at hand. I was not worrying about the look on his face; just having him there was enough for me, because he was one of us, the *Maighstir*, dead set against the unjust rule of the factor and the laird. And he had the education to put into words – words that could sting and exalt a man like the lash of the salt sea spray – the feelings of those who saw the land of their fathers being taken from them by the cunning of the law, and knew themselves to be without the learning to do more than make an angry swear.

Mr Nicolson nodded gravely to the sergeant. He did not look at me at all, but, as the policeman at my back let go of my jersey, took me by the arm and guided me into the classroom.

There were two men standing by the *Maighstir's* big desk. One of them, a large, heavily fleshed man, looking as

* Master.

if he had newly risen from the table after eating too much, I knew well enough by sight, having been trained since years to snatch the bonnet off my head the moment I clapped eyes on him. He was Major Traill, the laird's factor, a proud man, his importance pinned about him like a row of medals on his chest. The other man was a stranger to me. He was every bit as big as the factor but harder looking, firmer fleshed, with a great beak of a nose and dark eyes that seemed to burn right through you to your backbone.

The *Maighstir* cleared his throat. 'Superintendent Fleming has come all the way from Inverness to investigate a very serious matter. He has some questions to ask you, Alasdair. Answer truthfully, boy, the way you have been taught. And speak up.' He cleared his throat again, and let go of my arm.

'Sit down, boy,' the superintendent said, his voice not unkind, but no less frightening for that, with those piercing eyes at the back of it and that great beak of a nose sniffing for trouble. He pointed to a desk at the front of the room.

I sat down. Once there, feeling the iron frame of the desk cold against my bare feet, it was hard to believe that two years had passed – no, very near three – since I had ceased to be a scholar. I felt myself shrinking in stature; the hard-won years of my manhood slipping from me.

'How old are you, boy?' the superintendent said.

I passed my dry tongue along dry lips. 'Sixteen, sir,' I said.

He laid a sheet of ruled paper on the desk. 'Mr Nicolson tells me you were a good scholar.'

'Lacking a little in application, perhaps,' the *Maighstir* said quickly, 'but well above the average. I would have liked to put the boy through for a bursary, but with his father being crippled he was needed for work at home.'

'Get on with it, Fleming,' the factor said, the sneer in his smooth, sleepy voice emerging sharp as the claws of a cat. 'We are not here to discuss family histories.'

The tap, tap, tap of his riding-crop on the soft leather of his polished boot hit me as hard as if it had been my face taking the blows.

'I only . . .' the *Maighstir* began. He stopped as suddenly as he had started, frozen into silence by the factor's cold blue eyes, and I thought of the long winter nights I had spent in the kitchen of the schoolhouse, himself telling me that all men were created equal, and that in America it had been written so in their Declaration of Independence over a hundred years ago, and it could be the same for us if only we would speak and act like free-born men. My word, he had not been stopped so easy in his own kitchen, the *Maighstir*, with his sister knitting quiet by the fire, not daring to interrupt and make tea until he was done laying off his chest, and myself hanging on his every word – and the factor safe at home, miles out of earshot, in his big house on the other side of the hill.

'Write your name, boy,' the superintendent said calmly.

I picked up the pen on the desk, trying to stop my hand shaking, and dipped it into the inkwell. 'Alexander Stewart,' I wrote – Alexander being the English for Alasdair. When I had done, he said, 'Now, write General Kemball-Denison.'

I wrote 'General' and stopped.

'What is it?' he demanded, his great beak of a nose thrusting down at me.

'The general's name, sir,' I said. 'I – I am not sure of the spelling.'

He exchanged glances with the factor. The *Maighstir* cleared his throat again, but he did not speak.

'Well, make a try,' the superintendent said, his dark eyes stripping the flesh from my bones, boring deep within me.

I wrote 'Kembal' – K-e-m-b-a-l – and chewed at the

end of the pen, until I felt the factor's chill gaze on me, and added quickly: 'Dennison' – D-e-n-n-i-s-o-n.

The superintendent snatched the paper from me, and peered closely at it, the factor craning on tiptoe over his shoulder, no longer idly smacking his riding-crop against his boot. Then he took a sheet of paper from his tunic pocket and held it against the paper I had written on. He handed them to the factor and the pair of them went over to the window, speaking together so softly that I could not make out a word they were saying.

When they turned from the window, the superintendent smacked a sheet of paper down on the desk in front of me. It was not the one I had written on. 'You know what that is, don't you?' he said harshly.

I nodded.

'Well?'

'It is the paper you took out of your pocket, sir,' I stammered.

The factor's riding-crop thudded against the desk inches from my hands. 'No insolence, boy,' he shouted, 'or by God it will be the worse for you.'

'Read what is written there,' the superintendent said grimly. 'Aloud.'

I picked up the crumpled paper, trying to make out the scrawled writing. The ill-formed words jostled one another in an untidy straggle, as if the writer had been seized with a pressing urgency to get his message down on paper and be done.

'Go on,' the superintendent ordered.

'General Kembal Dennison,' I read slowly. 'Sir, I have Noticed in the Papers that you are determined to Remove these Men that have thrown down an enclosure you builded on their grazing land. You will hunt them down, you say, and when you have found them Remove them from their homes. Well, if you do as sure as there is a God in Heaven, if you Remove a single one of them . . .'

I stopped, not wanting to put my tongue to the words I saw before me. The factor caught me a stinger on the back of the hand with his riding-crop. I looked at the *Maighstir*. He was frowning at his boots.

'Go on,' the superintendent said.

I swallowed, and struggled on, gabbling the words, I was that eager to be done with it. 'If you Remove a single one of them there shall be Blood Shed. If I meet you Night or Day or anywhere that I get a Ball to bear on you I will strike you down. You are only a devil and it is to him you will go and the sooner the better. The curse of the poor and the Almighty be on you. I give you fair warning. Let these Poor men be or you Perish.'

There was a silence after that, a silence that seemed to go on and on and on, straining every nerve in my body until I could no longer control the trembling in my legs, and I was seized by a terrible need to make water. And all the time the superintendent's terrible dark eyes were boring into mine, and the only sound was the angry tap, tap, tap of the factor's riding-crop against his boot, and the hardest thing of all to endure was the silence of Mr Nicolson, the *Maighstir*.

Well, if they were waiting for me to say that I had written the letter threatening to do murder to the laird they would wait a long time, bad and all as the silence was.

'Did you notice the spelling of the general's name?' the superintendent said at last. His voice was low, friendly almost. 'It was wrongly spelled – the way you did it.'

I nodded, too dazed to do anything else, although, in truth, I had not noticed how the laird's name was spelled.

'What was your idea?' he said, still in the same quiet tone. 'Did you think you could frighten the general?'

'*Dhia*, no, not me,' I cried, finding my tongue again, my voice loud and shrill in my ears. 'As I am before God, it was not me wrote that letter.'

'Who, then?'

'I don't know.'

'Your father?'

'My father is not able.'

'Who, then?'

'I don't know.'

'Who pulled down the laird's wall?'

'I don't know.'

'You saw them at it.'

'No.'

Well, I am telling you, if the silence was bad, the questions were worse. They came at me non-stop, the factor joining in, too, and the pair of them getting wilder with every minute that passed. Before long they were shouting at me, thudding their fists down on the desk under my nose, the factor roaring that I would be spending the rest of my life in jail if I did not tell them what I knew. But I sang dumb, too scared to open my mouth at all, clinging to the truth that they could not hang a man for shaking his head.

I thought the questioning was never going to end but all of a sudden the superintendent called to the sergeant who must have been standing at the door all the time, and ordered him to take me out to the wagonette. The scholars were still there but there was no sign of Mairi, thank goodness, so she was spared the sight of me being taken off by the police.

A cluster of old wives, like a flock of eager black crows, had gathered by the bridge over the river, and my word they did not miss much, I am telling you. As the wagonette rattled over the bridge their long necks craned forward like cormorants in search of a fish. It was then that I saw Seumas Crubach. He was pushing a way through the cailleachs* to get a better view, his small, twisted figure bent low over his stick. He had never much of a colour at the

* Old women.

best of times, seeing he worked indoors all day crouched over pieces of cloth at his trade of a tailor, but his face was grey when he saw me in the wagonette with the police. He might well look grey, Seumas Crubach, for he knew that I knew he had written the letter threatening to kill the laird.

Chapter 2

Some men are born stupid. They may be clever enough with their hands but they never learn to use their heads. Seumas Crubach was like that. Give him a needle and thread, a scissor and a length of cloth, and he could fashion clothes that even the gentry would not scorn to put on their backs. But, my word, when it came to using the head the same fellow was lost. Indeed, it would take the like of Seumas Crubach to think he could threaten murder to the laird and not have the place crawling with police desperate to lay hands on one they could charge with the crime. And I could have kicked myself, for I should have guessed what he was about if I had used my wits.

It was the day the *Maighstir* asked me to see if the tailor had finished the new winter topcoat he was making for him that Seumas Crubach wanted to know how to spell the laird's name. I told him – wrongly, as it turned out – and he jotted the general's name down carefully on a scrap of paper, chuckling away to himself and enjoying a good scratch at the corns on his ankles, corns that came from sitting cross-legged every day in life, excepting the Sabbath, on his big work-table. When I was little he used to show me the corns on his ankles – monsters they were, too – saying proudly they were the mark of his trade, and that you could always tell a tailor from other men supposing he was standing naked before you. When I asked what he wanted with the laird's name, he said he was writing a letter that would put a stop to the general's big talk of carrying out evictions in the place. I had taken no heed, knowing he was for ever writing letters to the papers, and never getting any of them printed that I knew of. And I had thought no more of Seumas Crubach and his letter writing, not seeing danger coming from a poor cratur with a curve to his spine and one leg shorter than the other, who could only drag himself along with the aid of a stick, for all the world like an awkward crab out of water.

Not that I thought about him for long, now that I was a prisoner of the police. To tell the truth, it was the *Maighstir* who was in my thoughts as the wagonette climbed the twisting road that wound up the high pass between the hills, the horses straining themselves into a lather of sweat, every fresh bend no sooner rounded than the stretch of road we had just left was brought into view, directly below.

He had not been long in the place, the *Maighstir* – five years just – but it seemed to me that my life had started with his coming. He had given me books to read that but for him I would never have known had been written, and made me aware of a world beyond our island where men were free of the rule of the laird, and talked to me as an equal in a way that no man with education had ever done before. That was why I placed him far above other men of quality, like the factor, who would not have dreamed of giving me a word in passing, unless it was a swear for being slow in doffing my bonnet; and that was why I could not get over the shock of seeing him silenced by the factor in his own school, he who had taught me that free men should never be afraid of speaking out for their rights. The more you build a man up the greater the fall when the image you have made of him crumbles before your eyes, but it was hard for me to accept that I had seen the *Maighstir* – of all people – become of no more account than any paid servant of the factor who scurried to do his master's bidding like a trained dog. There was no denying it, though. My idol was in pieces – near as many pieces as the huge statue he had told me about, a statue of Liberty that was being taken to

America on board a French ship-of-war where it was going to be assembled outside the harbour of New York. It is easy enough, I suppose, to put together a statue, even one in three hundred and fifty pieces, but once the image of a man is broken it can never be made whole again.

I wearied my brain thinking about the *Maighstir* until my head ached, and I was that deep in thought I very near cried out in alarm when the sergeant suddenly put a hand on my knee.

'Well, boy,' he said, 'you have had plenty time for thinking, eh?'

I nodded warily.

His grip on my knee tightened. 'Take a tip from an old 'un,' he said, shutting one eye in a slow wink that was as false as the earnest expression on his face. 'Admit you wrote that letter and tell the general you did wrong.' He patted my knee. 'It'll be best for you in the end, laddie.'

We had crossed the flat table of high moorland and reached the west coast of the island. The road clung to the face of the hill, winding steeply down to the shore far below. Over the side of the wagonette, I could make out a long arm of the sea reaching in to an enclosed bay that was almost completely land-locked. It was as if a giant's boot, one with a sharply pointed toe, had stamped out a sheltered hollow in the heart of the towering hills. Fishing smacks rode peaceably at anchor in the bay, a flock of screaming gulls circling above them. The blue peat smoke from the croft houses lining the near shore lifted lazily on the still air. Somewhere down there was the factor's house; the laird's lodge had been swept away in the great flood of '77.

'Well, boy,' the sergeant persisted, 'what do you say?'

I was seized suddenly by a feeling of utter loneliness and despair. I had been falsely accused of a crime I had not committed and plucked from our township with as little ceremony as if I had been a bundle of worthless rags taken up on the back of a tinker. Now, I was about to be paraded through a strange village, in the grip of policemen, like any common thief. It all boiled up inside me so that I was past caring what I said. 'Ach, I am sick tired of questions,' I shot at him. 'I am not for answering any more supposing you keep on all night.'

The sergeant caught me by my jersey and shook me until my teeth rattled. He thrust his angry red face so close to mine that the sour breath and the stale, rank sweat of the man made me draw back in disgust. He thought I was afraid, and he fairly gloated at me. 'Tell that to the general,' he said, his mouth working as if he was making a good meal of the words. 'Aye, tell that to the general, boy, and see what will happen to you!'

The factor's house was as big as a kirk; a long white building with a high, slated roof. I was pushed into a room at the back and the door bolted behind me. The cold flagstones of the floor felt good against my feet after the heat and dust of the wagonette, and the whitewashed walls were that clean a spider would never have dared spin a web on them. A huge iron cauldron hung from a hook over the fireplace and a big mangle stood in the corner opposite the door. There was a scrubbed deal table under the high window and wooden wash-tubs about the floor.

I went to the window and stood on tiptoe looking out on a paved yard. The yard was bounded by a dry-stone wall, built into the rising ground at the back and thickly overgrown with mosses and ferns. Above the wall, the ground rose high in terraces, their steep banks clothed with trees and shrubs. There was a murmur of gently running water. I traced the sound to a tiny spring. It trickled down the wall into a stream coloured with late-flowering yellow mimulus.

I stood at the window for long enough, watching the shadows lengthen across the yard as the sun dipped in the western sky, straining my ears for a step at the door that never came. The only sound was the gentle splash of the spring into the stream, the song of the birds in the trees, the distant lowing of cattle on the hill, and the ceaseless clamour of the gulls in the bay.

I never heard her approach or the sound of the bolt being slid back or the door opening. She was in the room and had closed the door behind her before I wheeled round from the window.

We looked at each other for a long time, not speaking. I would not like to say which of us was the more surprised. She opened her mouth to speak and closed it again without making a sound, and stood with her back to the door, blinking at me as if I had two heads. For my part, I just stood where I was, gaping at her.

She had a proud nose on her, and she got it hoisted in the air, saying haughtily: 'Did you think you could frighten the general with a silly letter?'

Well, I am telling you, I was not having that from a girl who was no older than myself by the look of her, and I gave her a scowl that should have sent her packing there and then.

She brushed back a lock of black hair from her pale face – black as a raven's wing it was against the white of her cheek – and took a half-step towards me. 'Answer me,' she demanded, stamping her foot as if she thought I could be brought to heel like a puppy dog.

I looked down at my feet, stained with sphagnum moss and black with peat from crossing the bogs on the moors, itching something terrible where the peat had dried between my toes. I rubbed one foot against the other, not wanting to bend down and scratch.

'Don't you understand English?' she said.

'Aye, fine,' I said, and then, my anger getting the better of me, not caring supposing she was the daughter of the factor and would make straight for her father with my words on her lips the moment I was done, 'and I have had bigger ones than you at me. The superintendent o' police and the factor, and I am sick tired o' them and their questions, I can tell you. Besides, I never wrote any letter to the laird.'

'Why are you here, then?'

'Because I was the only one they could lay hands on. Every man in the place is away to meet Lachlann Ban off the steamer.' Seumas Crubach was not away, I thought, but the same one would have been fly enough to keep out of sight of the police even supposing he had not written the letter to the laird.

'Lachlann Ban?'

'A neighbour. He was coming home from Edinburgh. All the men in the place are away to meet him.'

'But why should the police pick on you?'

'If the laird gives an order to get a hold of a man you may be sure the police will not be slow in fastening on someone,' I said bitterly, 'even supposing there is only the one man in the place and himself with no word of what it is all about.'

'That's nonsense,' she declared. 'Anyway, you are not a man.'

'Well, I do a man's work.'

'You are only a boy,' she said scornfully.

'I am sixteen,' I said, 'and there is not much in the way o' work about a croft that I am not able for.'

'Where do you live?'

I told her the name of our township, and I knew by the look on her face that it was not the first time she had heard it. Sure enough, she said, 'Isn't that where the trouble was? A man sent to prison for attacking a sheriff officer?'

'Lachlann Ban,' I said, and I could not get the words out fast enough I was that eager to set her right, 'and he was trying to stop them putting an old woman out of her house because she could not find the rent and they put him to the jail for it.'

23

She said slowly, 'And so you all refuse to pay any rent now?'

'Aye, and no wonder,' I said hotly, 'seeing it is up three times since the general became laird, and the most of our hill pasture taken from us, and a rent wanted for the right to gather whelks from the shore, and another rent to be paid before peats can be cut, and drift timber to lie on the rocks waiting the pleasure o' the laird, and himself able to put us out of the place whenever he chooses, supposing he is not pleased.' I stopped to draw breath, and added: 'Why do you suppose so many folk have cleared off to America?'

'Why?' she said.

'Because there is none o' that in America. No lairds and factors and the like.'

'How do you know?'

'Because I have read books. Because it says in the Declaration of Independence that all men are created equal.'

'But they can't all be lairds,' she said coolly. 'You would have your superiors in America just the same.'

'Aye, but not lairds and factors.'

'Well, the names might be different.'

'There is more than the names different, I am telling you.'

'Mightn't they be worse, your new masters?'

'Ach, away. See you the crowd that has cleared out o' this place for America. And doing well for themselves, too.'

'How do you know?'

'They have written letters home. I have seen them. Many a one.'

'Would you like to go?'

'Me?' I said, startled, for it was a thought that had never entered my head.

'Yes. To America.'

'I was here all my days,' I said slowly, feeling somehow

24

that she had trapped me, and not knowing how best to escape, 'and many a one before me since generations – long before there was any word o' the general's name in this place.' I turned to the window, angry with myself; why, I knew not. A thrush had been perched on the sill. He flew off as I moved. 'You don't understand,' I said. 'You don't belong here.'

'No, I don't belong here,' she agreed.

But she did not say where she was from, although I had a good idea, because she spoke the same clipped sort of English as the factor. There was a silence. I looked down at my bare feet, suddenly conscious of the soft leather of her boots and the rich stuff her dress was made of and the crisp satin ribbon in her black hair.

'Do you always go barefoot?' she said.

I shook my head, feeling the colour rising in my face. She would be thinking I was without boots, and I had a beauty of a pair at home, oiled ready for the winter, with tackets that left clear prints on soft ground as good as a design by an artist, so good that you had to stop and feast your eyes on them.

'I like going barefoot,' she said. 'It's lovely feeling the grass under one's feet, all tingly. But Miss Butler says it is immodest – and dangerous if there is dew upon the grass.' She wrinkled her nose and made a face, the haughtiness gone from her in an instant, so that I wondered how I could ever have imagined so cold a quality about her.

'Who is Miss Butler?'

'My governess.'

I was not too sure what a governess was – some sort of servant, I guessed – but I did not let on.

She wrinkled her nose again. 'Miss Butler's a frump.'

I did not know what a frump was either, not having the Gaelic for the word, so I looked down at my feet again, rubbing them nervously one against the other.

She said: 'Do you live in a thatched house?'

I nodded.

'With the fire in the centre of the floor?'

I nodded again.

'And a hole in the roof to let the smoke out?'

'Aye.'

'Doesn't it sting your eyes?'

'What?'

'The smoke.'

'No.'

'It did mine. It made the tears run. I was only inside a thatched house once.'

'Ach, you would soon get used to it.' I looked round the clean white walls, thinking of the dirty, smoke-stained beams of our kitchen at home. 'It's awful homely,' I said, 'the peat smoke.'

'I couldn't see a thing.' She gave a little skip and giggled. 'There was an old woman sitting on a bench. I never saw her at all, and I tripped over her feet. She let out such a cry I nearly jumped out of my skin.'

I nearly jumped out of mine when I heard a woman's voice, close by, calling: 'Miss Fiona! Miss Fiona!'

The girl frowned and put a finger on her lips. She opened the door softly and gave me a quick wave. Then she was gone, as swiftly and silently as she had come. The woman called once more, and then there was silence again, only the distant crying of the gulls, the noise of the birds in the trees, and the low steady murmur of the spring in the wall.

After a while, I went across to the door. It was as I had thought, she had forgotten to secure the bolt – or perhaps she had not fancied making a prisoner of me. A darker thought crept into my mind. If she was the factor's daughter, perhaps she had run to tell her father everything I had been foolish enough to say to her, and had left the door off the bolt for the pleasure of seeing the waiting police pounce on me when I tried to make off. But there had been an honesty of purpose about her that would never have stooped to the like of that, an honesty that was so inbred it showed in the way she spoke and held her head and in the open, direct gaze of her dark eyes. I knew that full well but before I could think straight I had to banish the demon of doubt from my mind, a demon nurtured by fear and loneliness and self-pity at my plight. It was shame that cleared my mind, shame that I could have thought so ill of her. Well, come what may, I would never take the chance she had given me and slip out of that door and away. I would face them all first; the superintendent of police; the factor – aye, and the laird himself.

I stood by the window, watching the busy flutter of the birds in the trees, thinking all the time about the girl. She was unlike any other girl I had ever met before, and it was not on account of her fine clothes. There was a something about her that made you know she would never shrink from a word or deed because of what others might think or say; a sort of fearlessness that was more than being without fear. It was right enough that all men were created equal – of that I was sure – but I had a notion that a man would need to be on his mettle to be the equal of Miss Fiona.

The second time the door opened I was prepared for it, for I heard the slow, heavy footsteps approaching long before the handle turned. It was not the police, as I had expected, but the coachman I had seen threatening the scholars with his whip outside the school. He was a man well up in years with a sour turn to his mouth and a mean eye on him. His wits were no livelier than his step either, for he had taken a couple of paces into the room before he stopped and looked back suspiciously at the door. The sour mouth became as near contented as it would ever be. 'Some loon will pay for this when the major hears,' he said smugly. 'The bolt not shot on the door and never a man near. A pity I didna have the sense to try the door, says you, eh? Good on you, says I, or our bird would ha' flown. Well, well, wait till the major hears.'

All the time he was speaking, he was looking me up and down as if I had been so much stinking refuse cast on the shore by a high tide, and himself not knowing how to rid his nostrils of the offending smell. 'Mercy on us,' he exclaimed, 'have you not boots, and you going before the laird?'

'The laird must take me as I am,' I said, 'seeing I never made over of my own free will.'

He cuffed me for that, but I saw the blow coming and ducked, taking it on the side of the head. 'Haud your tongue,' he shouted, the Lowland accent stronger than ever, such a rage on him you would have thought I had spat in his face. He snatched a clean sack from a shelf by the door and made me wash my feet in the stream under the wall, muttering to himself as I dried on the sack that the country was going to the dogs, the youth not knowing their place any more, every ignorant Jock thinking himself as good as his master.

'Well,' he said, sucking his lips back from his stained teeth and spitting tobacco juice into the clear stream, 'it is you for the laird, ma bold wee laddie.'

My heart started to thump, for all my brash words of a few minutes ago, as he led the way through a stone-flagged kitchen. A white-haired woman as round as a barrel was slicing carrots into a pot on a huge range, a roarer of a fire going, the coals glowing that fierce I never saw the like outside a smithy. The woman never looked up, but a maid at the sink turned to gaze at me, wide-eyed.

I followed the coachman along a passage, the thick carpet lovely to the feet, and bumped into him when he stopped suddenly a yard or two away from a finely grained door, the wood that handsome I wanted to reach out and put my fingers to it.

'Stand straight before the laird,' he whispered hoarsely,

'and dinna fidget. And pay proper respect. A word out o' place and I promise you the feel o' my whip across your back. Now, wait here.'

He strode importantly to the door and tapped softly, but the swagger was gone from him when he answered the summons from within. I heard him say: 'The boy, Laird.'

He beckoned me, and I entered the room, trying to stop my tongue poking out over my dry lips.

The three of them were sitting around a dark, polished table – the superintendent of police, the factor and the laird – and supposing I had never clapped eyes on the first two I would have known at once which was the laird. He was the only one who was at ease. The other two sat like men who know their master's eye is upon them.

I don't know why but I had always thought of the laird as an old man, and it came as a shock to see that he was a man in the middle years with not so much as a speck of grey in the black of his hair and short, pointed beard. I got a bigger shock when he looked at me with the same open, direct stare as the girl I had spoken to so recklessly. Understanding dawned slowly as I looked into his eyes; saw the proud nose on him; his hair – black as any raven's wing. I felt the blood rush to my face with the realization that General Kemball-Denison, the laird, was the father of Miss Fiona.

Chapter 3

If only I had known she was the daughter of the laird I would have kept a still tongue in my head. Not that it was lies I had told her, but the truth is a luxury the poor can ill afford. That was easy seen when the Queen's Commissioners were in the place last year, seeking word of our grievances, and finding few who dared speak their minds for fear of what would happen once the Commission was gone from the island. And you could not blame the people for singing dumb, seeing their betters were in thrall to the lairds. I mind Lachlann Ban telling of the Free Church minister who spoke before the Commissioners for long enough, never saying a word about the hill pasture that had been taken from us to make sheep farms but giving long thanks to the laird for providing a site for his new kirk – and it a piece of rocky ground not fit to nourish a goat. That was the way of it, and that was why I was quaking as I stood before Himself, certain sure that his daughter must have carried my rash words to him, and a bitter reckoning was about to be made of them.

But the laird gazed upon me with a mild enough eye, and all he said was: 'Is this your writing, boy?' holding up the sheet of paper that bore my name and his own.

I nodded, too full of dread to get my tongue working; aware that this dark, bearded man, to whom my father was no more than a name on a rent roll, had the power to banish us all from the place if he took the notion.

'I am satisfied that it is not the same hand that penned this' – he flicked Seumas Crubach's letter with a disdainful thumb – 'extraordinary document, despite the fact that the incorrect spelling of my name, in both cases, is identical.' His gaze embraced the factor and the superintendent, and I could have sworn there was a gleam of laughter in those dark eyes. 'It is not uncommon for me to find my name appearing in a variety of guises. This particular vagary' – he flicked the letter again – 'is one which seems to be greatly favoured by all sections of society, the learned and the unlettered alike. As evidence of the origin of this ridiculous threat' – again the contemptuous flick of the thumb – 'I find it valueless. And potential assassins, gentlemen, if you will accept the counsel of one reared in the rough arts of war, are not usually found in the ranks of beardless boys.'

His gently mocking words were directed at the factor and the superintendent, and the pair of them were not pleased, I knew that by a quick glance at their set faces. The superintendent was wise enough to sing dumb, but the factor was fairly bursting to get a word in.

'You make light of a threat to your life, sir,' he cried, the moment the laird was done, 'but I would be failing in my duty if I did not seek to smoke out this vile nest of agitators and desperadoes, and prosecute them with the full severity of the law they have come to despise. And that boy' – he pointed a trembling finger at me, that puffed up with rage he could not keep his hand still – 'is at the centre of it all. His father is one of the ringleaders; a notorious agitator – the ruffian who engineered the destruction of the wall of the new grazing park, and the rest of the poor, ignorant fools too terrorized to withstand him. And he is at the back of the agitation to refuse to pay rent, hoping that his claim to be a veteran of the wars will incline you to leniency, sir.'

'Is this true, boy?' the laird demanded.

I could only stand and stare stupidly at him, the factor's words buzzing in my ears like a swarm of bees that refuse to be put to flight.

'Is this true?' he repeated, an impatient edge sharpening his voice.

'No sir,' I said miserably.

'The boy's lying,' the factor snapped.

The laird looked at him, and the factor said no more. Then it was my turn to face those calm, dark eyes, so like the eyes of the girl with the crisp satin ribbon in her hair. It was no wonder to me that the factor's tongue was still before them. My word, many a man with a lie on his conscience would have crawled into his tomb to get clear of those eyes. But my conscience did not hinder me. It was not lies – not by my way of it – to stand by your father and the ones you had known all the days of your life – the ones who fought the good fight to keep the land from the grasp of strangers with the English law at their backs, land that had grazed the cattle of the men of my blood since the days of the raiding Norsemen. My duty was to my own people, not the laird.

He looked at me for a long time, and I met his gaze as well as I was able, trying not to fidget under that direct stare. 'Loyalty to kith and kin,' he said at last, 'is not always an unblemished virtue, boy.' And with that said, he started in on me, never once raising his voice but the words striking home as if he had laid about him with a flail.

I was to go back and tell the people it was the word of the laird that the ruined wall of his new park was to be rebuilt, within the month, by themselves; that any withholding of rent would be dealt with by process of law and eviction, and that the commands of the factor were to be obeyed in all things. News of their lawless acts had vexed the Government in London, and no less a person than Sir William Harcourt, the Queen's Home Secretary, had told Himself that the power of the Crown would be brought to bear on the people if they did not desist and respect the law. And the power of the Crown meant the military; armed soldiers by the hundred. If the people persisted in their foolish defiance, the soldiers would be summoned to ensure that the law was upheld.

That was the message, and I had to repeat it back to him before he was satisfied that I had understood every word.

'Good,' he said, 'you can go now.'

I fairly scampered for the door, the need to set my feet on the road over the hill, and gain the freedom of the moor, so strong within me that I could not contain myself. But the laird's voice called me back – before I had reached the waiting coachman.

'Were you given a good dinner, boy?' he asked, that friendly I was afraid he was mocking me.

I sought to cover my confusion by pretending I had not heard aright, but his gaze had already shifted to the coach-man, and it was good, I am telling you, to see someone else squirming under those steady dark eyes.

'Mercy, Laird, I clean forgot about the laddie,' the coachman exclaimed. 'I was that busy wi' the horses I –'

'Forgot your own dinner?' the laird inquired, in a voice that cut to the bone.

'Well, no, Laird.' The coachman shuffled his feet, that desperate to be let off the hook it was in me to feel sorry for him. 'I'll see the laddie gets a bite this minute, Laird.'

'Do, Scobie. And it had better be a good "bite". When the boy has been fed – adequately fed, mind – you drive him home.'

'Aye, Laird.'

'And, Scobie . . .'

The coachman had turned to open the door. At the sound of his name, he was that quick in wheeling round you would have thought an invisible hand had reached out and seized him by the collar of his coat.

'Remember you are responsible for delivering the boy safely to his father's house.'

'Aye, Laird,' he said again.

He touched his hand to his forehead and pushed me out

into the passage. As he closed the door softly behind him, I heard the factor say, 'His father's a trouble-maker; one of the worst. With all respect, sir – and the superintendent agrees with me – I think we should . . .'

I never heard what he thought they should do, for the coachman hustled me along the passage to the kitchen, making such terrible swears under his breath I wondered what had possessed the man. To hear him, you would think he had been robbed of a meal instead of being ordered to see that I got one. In those days, I was ignorant of the ways of the world, and I was not to know that servants can be stiff with pride as well as their masters.

I got a topper of a dinner from the white-haired *cailleach* in the kitchen – pea soup, that thick you could near stand the spoon up in it; more butcher meat than I had seen at home in a twelvemonth, and a great plate of potatoes, all floury white, every one of them neatly stripped of its jacket. And, to cap it all, there was a beauty of a bread pudding. I never saw the like of that bread pudding. It was crammed just with currants and raisins, so that you had only to show the spoon to it and it fell apart.

It was a rare dinner, but I was not in the right trim to relish it. And it was not the sight of the coachman, glowering at me from his stool in the corner by the big range, that put me off my food. It was the thought of the factor having let slip in his rage that he knew all about my father – knew that he was at the head of every move against the laird – that spoilt my dinner on me.

After Lachlann Ban had been arrested all the men in the township made a compact that they would stand together as one; if one was seized by the police the rest would try to free him, even if it meant joining him in the jail. Whatever was done to oppose the laird would be done in the name of them all, and they would all put a hand to it. Right enough, there were some who were not terrible keen on the idea, but, as Lachlann Ban once said when he was feeling down in the mouth, where you have more than your shadow for company you may be sure you are within spitting distance of the faint-hearted. It was one thing, mind you, for some to be slow to make a move that might anger the laird and bring the police down on them; it was another story, by any reckoning, if someone in the place was busy peddling tales to the factor. We had suffered many a thing in the past, but never a traitor in our midst. And if there was a traitor in the place, who could it be?

In my mind's eye I saw all the familiar faces of the men in our township. One by one I dismissed them from my mind. But there was one I could not be rid of; his image remained obstinately focused in the centre of my thoughts. I did not say his name – not even to myself – for to have done so, a part of me protested in torment, would have been treachery to him. But how can you betray a betrayer, another part of me replied. And there was no answer to that.

I was still gnawing at the problem, like a dog at an old bone, as I climbed up alongside the coachman behind the four jet-black Highland ponies; that taken up with my thoughts I could have been getting into a dung cart for all the notice I took of the laird's shining coach. Indeed, we had rounded the hairpin bend high above the village before it came to me that I had forgotten to look and see if Miss Fiona was watching at a window when the coach pulled away from the house. Well, it was too late now. The factor's house was no more than a white blur, far below, in the gathering dusk; the great headlands forming the entrance to the bay, twin black walls against the evening sky. I looked down at the still bay and the house until they vanished from sight as the road bore inland.

The night was creeping in fast; the high moorland wreathed in a misty drizzle that hastened the light from the sky. I was thankful I did not have to make the journey alone on foot across this bleak waste of moor where many a traveller in olden times, so they said, had breathed his last. Mind you, I believe I would have reached home before the coach, at the rate we were going.

Once we were out of sight of the village, the coachman had reined in the ponies to a slow walk. At first, I had thought he was being good to them – giving them a rest after the long, hard pull up the steep hill road – but we had covered two miles or more at the same pace, and still he held them back.

I glanced at him out of the corner of my eyes. His jaws were going steady as he chewed at a plug of tobacco, but there was a something about the set of his shoulders, close hunched like a savage dog about to spring, that I did not fancy at all. He had never said a word since we left the house, and the silence, which had not bothered me as the coach bowled smartly through the village, laid cold fingers on my spine now that we were moving along the lonely moorland road – moving that slow you would have thought we had a body in the back.

'Is the laird staying for long?' I asked at last, saying the first thing that came into my head I was that desperate to break the silence that so oppressed me.

He shot me a suspicious glance, and leaned over the side and spat a stream of tobacco juice under the slowly turning wheels. 'The laird's more important things to see to than this god-forsaken place,' he growled. 'He is away in the morn's morn.'

'And Miss Fiona?'

Another suspicious glance, more hostile than the last, it seemed, to my anxious eyes; another stream of tobacco juice over the side. But he was civil enough; proud, in his way, I think, to be able to speak of the doings of the laird and his family.

'Miss Fiona's staying for a while, poor lassie. For her health.' He grunted. 'As if the like o' this place would improve a lassie's health.'

A group of sheep struggled up from their dry bed on the road and scampered away to the safety of the moor. The dismal cry of a whaup sounded through the mist. I shivered, feeling the cold drizzle soaking through the front of my jersey. The lowering clouds were closing in on us, gloomy and foreboding; the feel of winter strong in the chill night air on the high moorland.

'It'll be dark before you make back to the village,' I said.

He grunted, but made no move to urge the ponies to quicken their pace, sunk that deep in a brooding silence you would have thought the man was in a trance. For one wild moment, it was in me to leap off the coach, thinking it was either that or a ride by his side through all eternity, himself silent as a graven image through all the aeons of time to come.

Well, I am telling you, it is terrible altogether the fancies that can grip a man on the moor at night. I had to summon all the strength of will I could muster to rid my mind of them. I fastened my hands tight over my knees and resolved not to say another word until we reached the end of the road.

The coach trundled slowly over a wooden bridge, the loose decking rattling under the wheels. There was a short incline ahead. Beyond, the road dropped into a hollow, the rocky shoulder of the hill rising steeply on the right. On the left, the ground was flat, a favourite camping site of the tinkers. I would have given a lot for a sight of their tents, but there was only a patch of blackened grass, where an old fire had been, to show that they were ever there.

The coachman suddenly sprang to his feet and urged the ponies off the road. He swung the coach round in a wide circle, and I was almost tossed from my perch as it bumped over the tussocky grass and bounced back on to the road again. He reined the ponies to a stop, the coach facing the way it had come.

'Well, ma brave wee laddie,' he crowed, the triumphant sneer in his voice sticking to the words like treacle, 'this is where you use your feet.'

I gaped at him, too startled to take in the meaning of his words.

'Get off ma coach, you trash,' he shouted wildly. 'Off, d'you hear?'

'The laird said you were to take me home,' I retorted, wild at the sudden quaver in my voice.

'D'you think I am for carrying the like o' you to your very doorstep in the laird's own coach?' he cried. 'Make off, ye Hielan' stot, or I'll land ye such a dunt ye'll no' rise again in a hurry.'

As I rose to my feet, determined to stand him out, he lunged forward and caught me a blow in the chest before I was squarely set. I toppled off the coach, falling heavily on my back across the drain at the side of the road.

'On your way, trash,' he jeered at me. 'Back to the midden where ye belong.'

'Wait you,' I cried, tears of rage clouding my eyes, 'till the laird hears o' this.'

'Think ye the laird will tak' heed o' the like o' you, ye gomerel? Never the day!' He laughed fit to burst, and let fly a string of swears at me.

I scrambled to my feet, such a fury on me I was fit to claw him down from the coach. He reached for his whip, whether to bring it down on my back or to spur the ponies to a quick trot, I shall never know. There was a huge pat of cow dung on the road at my feet. It was dry enough to the touch but the brittle skin was only on the surface. I scooped it up and flung it at him before he could raise his whip. The dung caught him full on the side of the head, breaking over his face, and I am telling you that put a stop to the swears. By the time he had leapt down from the coach, I was bounding across the moor as fast as I could go. He started after me but he had no legs for a chase and it was not long before his shouted curses grew faint at my back.

I ran until I was near spent. But every time I slowed to a walk I would imagine I was hearing stealthy footsteps behind me, and take off again faster than ever. Twice I stopped dead, and jumped back in alarm, thinking the shadowy forms ahead were crouching figures. But each time they were only rocks, looking like the forms of men in the half-light.

I hurried on, running and walking – more running than walking, if the truth be told – until my breath was coming and going like the harsh pant of overworked bellows. When I heard a roar in the distance, I thought my ears were playing tricks on me, for I had lost my bearings. I fought down the panic that rose in my breast, and advanced slowly, straining my eyes for the sight of a familiar landmark. Sure enough, I recognized the bare face of rock rising steeply on my right; another hundred yards and I could see the gleam of the fall, thundering down through a narrow cleft in the rocks; the outline of the wooden bridge over the rushing stream, and the dark bulk of Domhnull the shepherd's bothy on a green mound below the road. I knew where I was now. Another mile and I would come to the pass where the road wound down to our township on the plain far below.

I quickened my step, and I was half-way across the bridge when a voice said: 'Well, well, it's yourself, Alasdair.'

I stopped in my tracks, my scalp prickling with fright. As far as I could see, there was not a living creature to be seen, and yet the voice had sounded loud in my ears, an echo ringing from the rocks above the road. I was of half a mind to turn and run back the way I had come, and I thought to myself if I hear it again I am off. Then I saw him, emerging slowly from the dark gable end of the bothy, where he must have been standing watching the road. His two dogs bounded forward, barking wildly, the moment their master moved. It was Domhnull, the shepherd, and, my word, if there were prizes going for keen sight the same fellow would not be able to get inside his door for the trophies.

I went on across the bridge, thankful that I had not taken to my heels, or I would never have been able to look him in the eye again.

'Come on in,' he said. 'I was after putting the kettle to boil.'

I ducked under the low lintel and followed him and his thrusting dogs into the single room of his stone-built bothy, and sat down on the rough wooden bench. He was not much of a hand as a carpenter, Domhnull, but I was glad enough to rest on his bench, I am telling you. Something tickled my heel. It was one of the dogs inching out from under the bench to sniff at my feet. Bare feet must have been a puzzle to them, because their master was always well shod.

Domhnull flung a handful of bog fir on the glowing peats of the fire, and the flickering flames licked up the sides of the big black kettle that hung from the pot hook, casting a cosy glow about the lime-washed walls. I stretched out my feet to the flames, and no king in his castle ever took his ease with more pleasure than I.

'A bad night to be late on the road, boy,' Domhnull said, breaking a peat across his knee and fitting it under the kettle. 'An awful chill in the air.'

'Aye, it's cold,' I said, still breathing hard.

He was crouched over the fire, and he glanced up at me, the bright flames gilding his head so that he looked like a figure in bronze I had once seen in a book the *Maighstir* had given me. He had the same crisp, curly hair and long nose and tight mouth. You would never take him for a first cousin of Seumas Crubach, whose face, poor man, was as twisted as his body.

'What ails you?' Domhnull said.

'I was running.'

'It's bad for a man – running.' He straightened his back, and sat down on the bench beside me. 'What was your hurry?'

'I was wanting home before dark.'

He nodded slowly, and took out a coil of tobacco and started to slice rings off it. I knew fine he would wait until he had got his pipe going before he said another word, and then he would edge the talk round to what was I doing on the road so late? and where had I been? and who had I seen? and what was doing with them? I never knew the like of shepherds for being eager to know the least thing about the doings of others. I believe it gives them something to think about when they are walking the hill with only their dogs for company.

Many's the time I made fun of Domhnull on the quiet, making him work at me for long enough before I would let on that I had seen Coinneach the piper making home from the inn in broad daylight with a stagger on him that was not canny, or Peigi, the daughter of Tomas the Elder, a terrible religious man and awful strict, creeping out on a Sabbath night to meet boys behind the peat stack at the end of her house. But I did not tease him tonight – did not even wait for him to get his pipe going – I was that thankful to have a man of my own kind to talk to in the Gaelic.

'Aye, I saw you in the wagonette,' he said calmly, when I told him that I had been seized by the police and taken to the factor's house.

'I never saw a sign o' you,' I said sourly, annoyed that my news had not come fresh to him.

'Ach, I was on the hill, boy,' he said, grinding the tobacco between the palms of his big hands. 'I had the glass on you.' He filled his pipe, taking his time about it. 'I was wondering what was on the go.'

Trust Domhnull to have seen me and never let on until I

came out with it myself. But he knew nothing about the letter threatening the laird's life, and that fairly put his ears back.

'Well, well,' he said.

I told him how the police and the factor had tried to make out that I had written the letter, and how the laird had squashed them and set me free.

'Well, well,' he said again, 'you were not slow getting clear o' them, boy. When the police get the like o' that in their teeth they are not for letting go at all, at all.'

He puffed steadily at his pipe, taking no heed of the kettle, and it putting out steam as hard as it could go, and myself that dry I was willing him to get up and make tea.

'There is not many in the place handy wi' the pen,' he said at last. And then, deep-set eyes fixed firm on my own: 'Who do you think it was made up the letter?'

It was on the tip of my tongue to say Seumas Crubach, I was that wild with the tailor for being so stupid, and I only just checked myself in the nick of time. Domhnull was shepherd to the tacksman* who had the grazing rights on the hill – the same hill that had fattened the cattle of our township when my father was a boy – and, as the tacksman was related to the factor, it might go badly with him if it came out that his cousin had threatened murder to the laird. And a shepherd, with no croft of his own to fall back on, would be worse off than a tinker if he lost his job and the bothy that went with it. I knew fine that Domhnull would think of these things, and brood about them for long enough, and maybe finish up by taking Seumas Crubach by the throat – and there was no profit in that for me. So I kept a tight grip on my tongue, and said I had no idea who the writer was.

Domhnull never said a word, just nodded in his own quiet fashion and got up to make tea. But I knew fine by

* Large farmer who holds a tack or lease of land from the laird.

the look in his eye that he was not believing me. It was only after he had reached over a length of the road with me, and we had parted, that the terrible thought came into my mind that he might be thinking I had told the laird who the writer of the letter was, and that was how the police had let me go.

I was so stricken with the idea that I footed it out without a thought of the dark of the moor all around. It was not until I reached the start of the narrow pass, the jagged peaks of the towering hills rising high above, blacker shadows against the black of the night, that I began to be aware of my surroundings. I stopped, certain sure there were shadowy shapes moving at the entrance to the pass where the road corkscrewed down, plunging between great walls of rock. But it was only an eddy of mist, drifting smoke-like across the pass; and the mist could do me no harm, seeing the gravel of the road bit sharp under my feet. My bare feet were better than eyes in the dark; they would guide me safely down the pass.

I looked around fearfully, and took a slow step forward. It was then that I heard it – the distant music of the pipes. I did not budge another inch. I stood stockstill, telling myself I was imagining things; that my ears were playing tricks on me; that it was the sough of the wind through the corries in the hills. But with every moment that passed the certainty grew within me that it *was* the pipes I was hearing.

The power of movement drained from me. I stood there, as if rooted to the ground, all the stories I had ever heard of ghostly pipers, returning from the dead to sound a last lament, racing madly through my mind. The skirl of the pipes was growing louder and louder, echoing wildly about the silent hills. But it was not a lament the piper was playing; it was a battle march! I tried to move, but my legs would not obey my will. I had to stand there, sweating helplessly, shaking as if the fever was on me.

It was when I heard the drunken shouts of warlike men, and knew for sure that the clansmen of old were out on a ghostly march, that I broke the spell that held me chained to the road. Scrambling behind a huge boulder, I flung myself flat on the ground, my hands clapped tight to my ears.

Chapter 4

I do not know how long I lay behind that boulder with my ears tight closed to the fearful noises of the night. When every heartbeat is sounding within your breast like the toll of a bell of doom, it is marvellous how a few brief minutes can be transformed into an age beyond belief. All I know is that when I summoned the nerve to raise my head – and it took long enough by my reckoning – the wild skirl of the pipes was no longer echoing round the hills. But I could hear something near as bad; the angry murmur of a great sea of voices, rising and falling like the wash of a strong tide on the shore when the noisy pull of the ebb is for ever struggling against the onward surge of the incoming sea. I got to my knees, cold hands clutching the cold face of the boulder, straining my ears to catch a word that would tell me if the language they spoke was mine.

A deep, booming voice rang out above the clamour, that loud and clear I heard every word.

'*Seas gu Dluth ri Cliu do Shinnsir!*'

There was no mistaking the boom of that voice; a voice so unlike its owner that strangers hearing him speak for the first time could scarce forbear to keep from their face a look of wonder. I knew fine it was Seumas Crubach speaking.

'Stand fast for the rights of your forefathers!' he cried once more. And again; and again; and again – repeating the old motto like a chant.

There were excited shouts of, '*Sin thu!*' '*Sin thu, 'ille!*' '*Seasaidh! Seasaidh!*' And the music of the pipes burst out again, wilder and louder than ever; music fit to make giants

45

of weaklings and armour them to brave fire and flood and steel; music that no longer struck terror in my heart since I knew now who was at the fingering of the chanter.

I ran back from the pass, stumbling over the moor to a grassy shoulder of the hill that fell sheer to the plain, overlooking the winding road below. Once I gained the top, I laid eyes on them – and, my word, I never thought I would ever see the like.

An army of men was on the march up the road, the ones at its head bearing flaming torches of pitch, and near every man carrying a smouldering peat to light his way, so that it looked like a long ribbon of fire mounting the pass. The flaming torches disappeared from view into the narrow mouth of the pass, but I could still see a long line of glowing peats coiling upwards like the tail of a fiery dragon.

The music of the pipes resounded from the bare rock of the pass, and I turned my back on the ones below to see the leaders gain the open moor. They streamed out of the rocky defile, Coinneach the piper at their head, such a rare swagger on him you would have thought he was heralding the path of kings. Then came my father, his empty right sleeve flapping loose at his side, and Lachlann Ban; not a big man at all, Lachlann Ban – shorter than my father, and he was not big – but such a strength and power in the very step and bearing of him that you never noticed his lack of inches, and it always came as a surprise to discover that men you have thought to be much smaller than him were really a head higher. Both Lachlann Ban and my father were dwarfed by Colla the smith – a right monster of a man, Colla – with little Seumas Crubach perched high on the great spread of his shoulders. And behind them strode score upon score upon score of men, some carrying flails and others gripping stout sticks and one with a scythe over his shoulder.

Dhia, it was a sight great to behold, the people gathered in strength and unafraid; and to know that it was for me they had rallied. I ran to meet them, shouting I know not what, I was that caught up in the excitement of it all.

My father got his good arm round me and hugged me tight. If he had not lost his right arm fighting the Russians at the siege of Sebastopol, I believe he would have cracked a rib on me. What with the squeeze he gave me, and Lachlann Ban thumping me on the back, and the hum of eager voices all around, the most of them working at me with questions, I was too harassed to get a single word out.

It was Seumas Crubach who silenced them, poking about him with his stick from his high perch on Colla's shoulders, and crying in that deep, deep voice of his that you felt should have been issuing from the throat of a man the size of the smith: '*Ist! Ist! Ist!*' And Seumas Crubach it was who passed on my news as I spoke, his words taken up by those around him who were not hearing me, and whispered back from mouth to mouth until all that great concourse was informed of the will of the laird. I did not say a word about the letter threatening murder to Himself, seeing it had come from our township, and there were strangers listening who would have carried news of it far and wide to the shame of us all.

The moment I was done Lachlann Ban forced a way through the press of people to a flat table of rock. He scrambled up on it, and hauled me up after him. Eager hands seized my father, hoisting him off his feet and lifting him alongside us. Lachlann Ban spread his arms wide, and the multitude hushed that quick you would have thought they had a strong preacher standing before them ready to make known the Word of God.

'Well,' he cried, 'you have heard the word o' the laird, not from his own lips but from the lips of Alasdair – a boy o' sixteen, and himself taken by the police and held at the factor's the whole day, waiting the pleasure of his master, and then set free to walk the hill in the dark o' night. And all that we might know the will of the laird! I say the laird

47

should have shown face himself, or sent his goat-toothed factor. Either one of them would have done. They would have got an answer from us that would have put a stop to . . .'

The rest of his words was drowned in a great roar of assent from the crowd. As the roar slowly dwindled to a low rumble of voices, I took the chance to whisper to my father that the laird had given orders for me to be taken home in his own coach, and it was his servant who had put me out to walk.

But my father was not pleased. 'Servant or laird,' he said angrily, 'it is all one, boy. They had no right to take you from home and that is all about it.'

I made to speak, but he motioned me to be quiet. Lachlann Ban had spread his arms wide again.

'Aye, we would have given the laird an answer,' he went on, not shouting at all, but his voice reaching out to the farthermost ring of listeners, sparking them all with something of his own fiery purpose, 'and that answer would have been that we stand fast on our ancient rights. I say no to the laird; no to the raising of a wall that would rob us of grazing land that was ours since olden times; no to the payment of a rent that has doubled since the days of the old laird, and our land shrunk near by half; no to obeying the commands of a factor who would grind us down worse than the beasts o' the field. And if the laird talks of obeying the law, I say there is no law in this place.' He seized my wrist, holding my arm on high. 'What like a law is it that would countenance the lifting of a boy from his home because the laird wills it, and him the son of a man who gave his right arm fighting for his country?'

There was another roar from the crowd; a deep-throated roar, and so fired by anger that it went on and on. I thought they would never stop, but Lachlann Ban had them hushed the moment he raised his hands again.

'The laird's will and the word o' the factor, that is the

law in this place,' he cried, 'and we are no better than beasts o' burden until we clear it from our backs and stand up as free men. Let him summon his soldiers! What can he do but hide behind their bayonets? Good grief, he cannot slay the lot of us for wanting to be free. And free we shall be. If only we stand fast, we shall be the rock on which the laird shall perish.'

'Stand fast!' the crowd chanted as one, the words booming out across the dark moor like the beat of a mighty drum. 'Stand fast! Stand fast!'

There were some among them who were all for marching on the laird and taking him out of his bed, although Lachlann Ban and my father were against such a move. It was a piece of foolishness, right enough, but it was not so much the whisky in them talking as the noise and strength of the gathering that had gone to their heads – that and Seumas Crubach. If ever a man was roused to a frenzy it was the tailor. Seeing his dark, twisted face in the flickering light of the smoking torches, he put me in mind of a demon of olden times, and it was terrible to watch the way he prodded Colla to move to a fresh stance in the crowd, as if the smith was of no more account than a dumb ox and himself the undisputed master. Perched high on Colla's broad shoulders, he could look down on them all for once, and I believe that had a worse effect on him than a jug of whisky. The tailor never tasted strong drink, and, my word, it was as well, seeing the way he slashed the air wildly with his stick, and boldly mocked those who were not eager to march, saying they should stay quiet by the fire and let the *cailleachs* wear the trousers since they had cast away their manhood. And when he was not mocking he was goading them on with stories of the women of The Braes; the Amazons, who had stood fast against the charge of Sheriff Ivory's men, hurling rocks down on the police from the heights above Balmeanach.

There was a devil in the tongue of Seumas Crubach, I am

telling you, and I believe the most of them would have stormed off to confront the laird at his bidding, no matter what Lachlann Ban and my father said to dissuade them, had it not been for Colla the smith. Seumas Crubach was fairly laying off his chest, the stick going good style, when the smith suddenly ducked his head and threw him clean off his shoulders. The tailor landed on his back in a patch of sphagnum moss, and the sullen muttering of those he had inflamed to mischief was swept away in a great cleansing burst of laughter.

'Ach, I am sick tired o' you and your noise, Seumas,' the smith said to him, as he lay on his back in the wet, too shaken for the moment to give tongue. 'Calm yourself, boy, or it is you for a night on the moor.'

The tailor fairly spat with rage at that, cursing something terrible, and groping about wildly for his stick. No man likes being made to look foolish, but Seumas Crubach did not have the sense to realize that there are times when a man must sing dumb if his wounded pride is to be spared further suffering. A spate of swears flowed from him, some of them as long as your arm – and the longer the swears, the louder were the howls of delighted laughter that greeted them.

Colla snatched up the tailor's stick and threatened to break it in two. 'Not another word, mind,' he warned, 'or the stick is in pieces.'

That put a stop to the swears, for his stick was as precious to him as the legs of other men. And with Seumas Crubach silenced there was no word now of marching on the laird, which was as well seeing the time it took us to make down the pass to the start of the croft lands below, and many a one in the gathering miles from home.

We had shed the bulk of the men from the other townships at the bottom of the pass, and we parted from those who came from the west side of the river at the bridge. But there was still a crowd at our back, all of them men belonging to our own township, when we left the road above the bridge and took the track across the croft to our house.

My mother was standing at the door, not pleased at all by the look of her. She backed into the kitchen before us, taking a quick feel at my sodden jersey, making a quicker sniff, and saying the *Maighstir* had been to see if I was home, but that was hours ago, and it was far too late now to get word to him, and what a pity it was that he was away to bed not knowing I was back and Himself maybe thinking she had not bothered to send word – all in such a scolding tone you would have thought I had been out on a jaunt for my own pleasure.

But she was like that, my mother, always humbling herself to those, such as the *Maighstir*, who she thought were above her. Mind you, there was more to it than that. She was the daughter of a *Ceistear*;* a godly man, one who took no heed of the things of this world, so certain sure was he of the everlasting glory that was to come. My father used to say it would not have put the *bodach*† up or down supposing everyone in the place had to scratch a living from the shore picking limpets from the rocks, provided they knew their Catechism. Certainly, he would no more have dreamed of saying a word against the laird than he would of letting a swear pass his lips. And my mother had the same submissive nature to the outside world, and it angered her that her family could not plough the same quiet furrow as her father, who had died, as he had lived, without a single complaint on his lips.

'Ach, supposing,' I said. 'The same one will know soon enough that I am back.'

'Good grief, is that the way to speak o' the *Maighstir*, boy?' she flared at me. 'No wonder the police were after making off with you if that is the tongue you were using on them.'

* Catechist.   † Old man.

'Be quiet, woman,' my father said, conscious of the men crowding the door at his back. 'See who is here! Lachlann Ban! And himself given a send off from Edinburgh fit for a king! Six pipers and a great crowd wi' banners was after seeing him off at the station. In Edinburgh, mind! Did you ever hear the like o' that?'

But my father's enthusiasm lit only the shadow of a smile on her face, and there was no great warmth in the way she took Lachlann Ban's hand and welcomed him home. I knew fine she had no fancy for Lachlann, thinking him an idle trouble-maker. And she was not the one to make much of a crowd with banners – not even an Edinburgh crowd. The thought of a full meal chest in the house would have excited her more. Mind you, she had her own favourites, the *cailleach*. There was a difference in the way she fussed over Seumas Crubach; prodding Mairi, who was curled up asleep on a corner of the bench, to rise and make room for him. It was a wonder to me why she had such a notion for the tailor, and himself with swears that would have put her father near off his head, although the same one was fly enough to watch his tongue whenever she was handing him barley cakes and asking was the tea to his liking.

Still and all, it was good to be home again; good to be back in the kitchen and it crowded with men – the air fairly crackling with talk there were that many tongues on the go; good to see the flames from the fire, set cosy in the centre of the floor, coiling up the big iron soup pot that hung secure from its smoke-blackened chain; good to watch the peat smoke drifting slow about the room, the scent and feel of it that strong in my nostrils I would have known I was home supposing I had been blinded; good to see the bright eyes of my little brother Seoras peeping shyly round the corner of the ragged blanket that hid his bed in a dark recess in the wall; the bed he shared with me. My word, it would be great to stretch out on the

52

mattress of soft straw, with the dying peats glowing red in the dark, and Seoras warm beside me.

A hand gripped my knee, and a deep voice said, 'You were gone a terrible time, boy, just to gather a handful o' words from the laird.'

I looked into the small brown eyes of Seumas Crubach, all thought of sleep gone. 'Ach, there was more to it than a message from Himself,' I said loudly. 'What took the police over was a letter threatening murder to the laird if he put a single one of us away from the place. And they were after trying to make out it was me had written it.'

He was cool, Seumas Crubach, I will say that for him. He never batted an eye, just gripped his stick a shade tighter, and stared straight back at me. The rest of them all started talking at once, hurling questions at me as hard as they could go, wanting to know what like a letter it was, and expecting me to be able to repeat it word for word. All but Lachlann Ban. He had pulled off his bonnet and was running the flat of his hand over his head, that deep in thought he had not a word to say. Nor me either when I saw that his thick thatch of straw-coloured hair was cropped close to his head. They must have shorn him in the jail, and without his mop of hair he looked older – different altogether; frightening almost, as if he had lost the kindness in him as well as his hair.

He clapped his bonnet back on his head, and said angrily: 'If I had the clown that wrote that letter I would break him in pieces.' He thumped his clenched fist into the palm of his hand, smiting it such a blow that it made a crack like a pistol shot. 'If there is word o' murder being done, Sheriff Ivory could call in the military tomorrow and clear us all out o' the place, and not a voice would be raised against him in the length and breadth o' the land.' He let his words sink in, looking round the room at them all; and he had a savage eye on him, I am telling you. 'Murder is it? There will be murder done, right enough, if I lay hands on the one that wrote that letter!'

I believed him. One look at that tight-lipped mouth, and the flaming anger in those flinty blue eyes, and you would know he was fit for murder, if the cause was just. So I sang dumb. Not so Seumas Crubach.

'Ach, it is easy seen who was the making of that letter,' he declared boldly.

Every one of them shot a 'Who?' at him.

He took his time answering, looking at them all in turn – at Colla the smith, Iain Beag, Martainn, Eachunn Ruadh, Padruig, Tomas the Elder – his hands clasped tight; that solemn you would have thought he was at a prayer meeting – Somhairle, Coinneach 'he piper, my father and Lachlann Ban. And all the time I was sitting by his side, near bursting with impatience, and marvelling at the nerve of him.

'Ailean Mor,' he said, at last. 'The same fellow is daft enough for the like o' that.'

Ailean Mor was an old man who stayed by himself in a ruin of a house close by the river, with only a goat for company – and a billy at that, the stench off the beast something awful in the rutting season. All the *bodachs* said he had been a great scholar in his day, able to read English and himself never inside a school, but he was blind of an eye now and not right in the head, taking many a queer turn when the moon was full, walking by the river in the dead of night, singing psalms and calling on sinners to repent. There were some who said he had foretold the coming of the great flood that had swept the laird's lodge into the sea, so you may know he was the sort of man people will believe anything of – and the tailor had been fly enough to fasten on that.

Indeed, the words were no sooner off Seumas Crubach's tongue than everyone was agreeing with him, some of them making out that they had thought of Ailean Mor before he opened his mouth. Well, it was not for me to let on that I knew better. I was not wanting to see the wee man stretched out on the earthen floor at my feet, Lachlann Ban's big hands at his throat, choking the life out of him. There was one thing sure, he was not likely to make the same mistake again. Besides, I had more important things to speak of.

My father saw me looking at him, and he must have read what was in my mind, because he said: 'Well boy, what more have you to say? It is not good, I know fine – so out with it.'

'It is about yourself, *Athair*,'* I said. 'The factor got that wild with me he was not heeding his tongue. He let on that he knew it was yourself had taken the lead in pulling down the laird's wall. And he knows fine you are the one who put round the word to keep back the rent. Someone is after . . .' I hesitated, wondering how best to get the ugly words off my chest.

Lachlann Ban had risen to his feet. The words fairly shot from him. 'Betraying us to the factor, is it?'

I nodded.

I have said that Lachlann Ban was not a big man, and neither he was, but seeing him standing there – balanced that easy on his toes he could have moved as swiftly to his left as his right, as quickly back as forward – it was not his size you were aware of but the lithe power of his body. If I had been the traitor, I would rather have faced Colla the smith, big and all as he was, than the like of Lachlann Ban.

The *cailleach* was the first to speak, and herself not the one to interfere in men's talk. 'I knew fine this carry-on would be the ruin of us,' she said, the words coming out with a strangled sob at the back of them.

'*Ist*, woman,' my father said absently, too taken up, I think, by the thought of treachery to be angry with her.

'But who?' Tomas the Elder demanded. 'Who, of our own, would betray us?'

* Father.

'Why should the traitor be one of our own?' Seumas Crubach said, his words fanning to life all the dark thoughts that had smouldered for so long at the back of my mind. 'For any favour, are there not incomers in the place?'

He brooded, his chin resting on his stick, sharp eyes downcast for once, intent on the red shell of the fire. The *cailleach* nudged Mairi, and she got up and fetched fresh peats. Nobody spoke.

'I can think o' one right off,' the tailor said at last, looking up and meeting Lachlann Ban's eyes, 'and the same one is at meetings often enough wi' the factor.'

'What meetings?' Lachlann Ban wanted to know.

Seumas Crubach scrubbed his chin on the crook of his stick. 'Meetings o' the School Board. The factor is chairman, and there is many a thing the chairman o' the School Board could do for a man who kept him fed wi' news of what is going on in the place.'

I almost blurted out the name Seumas Crubach had been careful to withhold, such a rush of anger rose within me at his confirmation of my own inmost thoughts. But my father was there before me. '*Dhia*, not the *Maighstir*?' he cried.

There was a long silence, every one of them busy with his thoughts. I knew fine what they were thinking: how could the *Maighstir*, who was never present at our gatherings, feed news to the factor unless he had got it from one of us?

None of them knew him well enough for that. They all looked upon him as an incomer, for he had not been five whole years in the place, and in our township no man is ever free with his tongue to an incomer. To tell the truth, the most of them were that shy of him they were not able for more than a word about the weather supposing they came face to face with him. Not one of them ever went near the school-house unless they were scrubbed and shaved, with a shine on their boots fit for a Communion Sabbath, and then only if they were desperate to get a letter written.

I knew the *Maighstir* better than any of them, and it is a terrible temptation, when you are friendly with a man your elders regard with awe, to seek to strengthen the bonds between you by matching confidence with confidence. That was how it came about, when the *Maighstir* told me he was busy writing Mr MacKenzie of the *Celtic Magazine* in Inverness giving him news – on the quiet, you understand – of how ill-used we were by the laird, that I was not slow in telling him of everything that went on. The *Maighstir* had sworn me to secrecy, saying it would be bad for him if word got out that he was in communication with Mr MacKenzie, our great champion on the mainland, and it had seemed only just that I should return the trust he showed in me by speaking freely to him. But that had been in the snug kitchen of the school-house, no suspicious eyes on me there, only his sister, Ruth, smiling quiet in her chair, the kettle putting out steam on the glowing hearth, and myself eager to show that I was as open as the *Maighstir* with my secrets.

Tomas the Elder said: 'Ach, who would be telling the *Maighstir* things that could destroy a man, and himself a stranger in the place?'

'The same one is not a stranger to this fellow,' Seumas Crubach retorted, prodding me in the chest with a bony finger. 'Who comes running to me every other day to find is the *Maighstir's* new coat ready?' Another prod in the chest. 'This one. Do you think this boy' – another prod – 'would be wise enough to keep a still tongue supposing his friend the *Maighstir* was on at him for news?'

I had been gazing down at my feet, and when I looked up I was conscious that every eye in the room was on me. It is bad enough facing the hostile stare of strangers, I am telling you, but when those you have known all the days of your life look upon you with distrust it is fearful altogether.

And all at the bidding of a poor *truaghan** whose envy of
these who were whole made him reckless of the mischief he
created! A surge of anger at Seumas Crubach swept over
me, clearing my mind something wonderful, so that I saw
in a flash what he was getting at and why. He had no proof
that the *Maighstir* was working against us – it was spite
just; the spite that made him slow in finishing work for any
man of importance, so that he would attend to the needs of
a tinker rather than hasten to the bidding of the tacksman
or the minister or the *Maighstir*; the spite that could not
accept the *Maighstir* being friendly with the like of me
unless he stood to gain by it. And by putting me in the
wrong he knew that I could not accuse him of writing the
letter to the laird for the rest of them would never believe
me now.

'Well, boy,' my father said, a mixture of anger and
anguish curdling his voice, 'is it yourself has been babbling
to the *Maighstir*?'

I put on as bold a look as I was able, meeting his eyes
squarely, 'Not me,' I declared, the lie forming so swift it
was off my chest before I had time to reckon the consequences. 'If the *Maighstir* has been feeding the factor wi'
news it was not from me he heard it.'

* Poor creature.

Chapter 5

I managed to keep out of sight of the *Maighstir* for two whole days, but not an hour of those days went by without Himself being deep in my thoughts. Time and again, I went over everything that had been said in our house, after I had lied my way out of trouble; as if, by sifting the dross from the talk, the truth concerning the *Maighstir* would be revealed to me. But it was not that easy. They had talked themselves dry about him, near half of them – and my father was one – maintaining that he would never spy for the factor, and the rest certain sure that he was the very one who was fit for it, since it would profit him to gain the favour of the laird. But they were no wiser at the end of the night, for all their talk, and neither was I. All I knew for certain was that the *Maighstir* had been careful not to say a word in my favour to the superintendent; and the factor had known that it was my father who had carried on the struggle against the laird after the jailing of Lachlann Ban. Mind you, that was enough to make me join the ranks of those who proclaimed him a spy, but I could not tell them they were right without revealing that I had betrayed their trust and exposed my own father to the venom of the factor.

Many's the time I thought of marching boldly into the school-house, and telling him what I had heard the factor say, in the hope that he would be shamed into showing the truth on his face. I thought about it, right enough, but I never did it. To tell the truth, I lacked the courage for the like of that. Indeed, I would never have gone near him if he had not sent word by Mairi that he wanted to see me urgently. Even then, I held back until Friday night, when Lachlann Ban and the rest of them were away to a meeting in the next township, and there was less chance of anyone seeing me slip into the school-house.

Miss Nicolson must have been watching for me. She met me at the door, all smiles. 'Come away in, Alasdair,' she panted softly, her mouth that pursed it was a wonder to me the words managed to escape. 'Duncan will be along presently. He is busy in his study.'

She always spoke in a breathless whisper, as if there were hidden listeners all around desperate to know what she was saying, and she always called him Duncan when speaking of him to me. I often used to wonder what she would say if I put his name off my tongue in the same familiar fashion. For my part, I never called him anything at all, for I knew him too well to 'sir' or 'Mister' him, and I never had the nerve to come right out with his first name, although there were times when I thought both of them would have liked me to. Names are queer things, and not only the names of people. I used to marvel at my own nerve in going to a house where a man had a study, and it was a long time before I discovered that it was just a room at the end of the lobby, no different from any other except that he did his writing there.

Miss Nicolson fussed around, settling me into a chair, saying: 'Och, it was shocking the police coming like that and the school having to be cleared for them. A disgrace for a place of learning to be used in such a way. Duncan was not pleased at all. And as for taking you away, poor laddie! I was vexed. Truly, I was. I could have wept when I saw them putting you into the wagonette. Indeed, I could.'

She bent over me, patting my arm and making little clucking noises, for all the world like a hen that is threatening to go broody. I tried not to look at the line of dark hair on her lip, Mairi's joking about her having a better moustache than the *Maighstir* strong in my mind, but she was that close to me I could not keep my eyes off it. 'And your mother, poor soul,' she went on. 'Duncan said she was distracted. And no wonder. It was too bad – too bad.'

I thought the clucks would never stop, but he came in himself then, and that quietened her. I knew at once by the way he clapped me on the back and brayed a loud welcome – he who was very near as quiet as his sister until he got worked up about the rights of man – that something was on his mind.

Mind you, he tried hard not to show it, saying briskly, 'Where have you been hiding, boy? We were expecting you days ago; eagerly awaiting news of your – ah, adventure.'

'Indeed,' his sister assented.

'Ach, I was busy lifting potatoes,' I said lamely, watching him as he took up a stance in front of the fire.

He was a tall man, the *Maighstir*, but terrible thin, with a long, bony face and big bony wrists and hands. I never laid eyes on those hands of his without thinking that they looked more able for a spade than a pen. But the rest of him had the stamp of a scholarly man – the stooping shoulders, and the pale face, and the habit he had of going back over a word that pleased him, and rolling it round his tongue, as if he was savouring the taste and finding it sweet.

'Did they treat you well?' he said.

'Aye, well enough.'

'And did you see the laird?'

I nodded.

'What did he say to you?'

'Ach, not much.'

He fingered his thin moustache. 'The general is a kindly man at heart,' he announced, speaking as if they were old friends, and me the one who knew fine he had hardly ever clapped eyes on the man.

'Aye, he is nice enough,' I said.

'Yes. I am sure he is.'

He cleared his throat. The silence was that awkward, I got a terrible tickle in mine, and when I held my breath to be rid of it an awful itch started in my back. I did not know where to look.

'I wanted to see you, Alasdair,' he said suddenly, 'to explain.' He plucked at the shaven skin of his neck, frowning up at the high plaster ceiling. 'The other morning at the school,' he went on, his pale eyes on my face now – bulging eyes, for ever blinking, as if surprised by what they saw, 'I was afraid you might not understand. You see, Major Traill, the factor, is chairman of the School Board, and – well, to put it in a nutshell, I am the servant of the Board. You understand?'

I had a good idea, so I said, 'You mean you have to do what the factor says?'

He gave a little smile that took in his sister, and she smiled back obediently at him. There was one thing sure, he would not lack an admirer so long as she was about the place.

'Not quite, Alasdair,' he said. 'I confess, boy, to an independent mind, answerable only to my conscience and my Maker. Outside the school, you understand. Within the bounds of my duties, I must take due cognisance of the Board. A man in my position has to walk with care for the road through life is pitted with snares – yes, pitted with snares for the unwary. It would not do for me to appear to take sides. Had I spoken rashly in your favour – and my views were not invited – it might have appeared that I was trying to obstruct the course of the law. You know that I favour a redress of the people's grievances, but if the person of the laird is threatened with violence – violence of the most barbarous' – he paused, looking up again at the ceiling – 'the most *barbarous* kind – it is my duty to stand firm on the side of law and order.'

'But it was not me wrote that letter,' I burst out.

He held up a long, bony hand. 'Patience, boy. I was aware of that at the time. But if I had intervened and convinced the superintendent of your innocence you might not have grasped the full gravity of the situation. Threats of violence – murderous violence – cannot be tolerated in a civilized society such as ours, and I fear it will go badly for you all if the culprit is not swiftly apprehended and brought to justice. If this is done, I am confident that the laird will look favourably upon the just complaints of the people, and remedy many of them without further agitation. One thing only is needed to put an end to the strife and that is the name of the wrongdoer.'

I did not take in everything he had said, but I was not so slow that I could not grasp what he was about. If he could succeed, where the superintendent and the factor had failed, and produce the name of the one who had threatened to kill the laird, that was him secure for life, and his advancement made easy. Well, if he was fit for that he was fit to feed the factor with any news he had got from me. I had no doubt now where the factor had secured his information. And that made me all the more determined not to sacrifice Seumas Crubach, stupid and all as he was, so that the *Maighstir* could bask in the sunshine of the laird's favour.

He took a turn across the hearth, his hands clasped tight behind his back. There was no stopping him now that he had got going. 'Believe me, Alasdair,' he said earnestly, 'I have the just cause of the people at heart, and I can see what damage is being done to that cause by senseless threats of violence. It will shock your most powerful sympathizers into silence. Men like Mr Fraser-Mackintosh, a Member of Parliament and a Queen's Commissioner. Men like Mr MacKenzie, of Inverness, who has ventilated the people's grievances in the pages of his worthy journal. And if their restraining hand is withdrawn, you will be led from one folly to another by ignorant hotheads who will plunge you all into utter ruin.'

I knew fine who he was getting at – Lachlann Ban. Because Lachlann Ban was without much schooling, the *Maighstir* thought he was not fitted to be a leader of men. That was nonsense just. Supposing a man could spout Latin and Greek by the yard, it would not add a single acre of land to our township, and that was our problem. And it was the land Lachlann Ban was schooled in; and there was little he did not know about the people who lived on the land, and what they needed in the way of more ground to be able to raise their crops and cattle, and provide for their families without fear of one bad harvest bringing famine to their door.

All of a sudden, I felt trapped. It was no longer me and the *Maighstir* close-knit in comradeship and the rest outsiders. That had been a dream; a dream fed by my own vanity. Good grief, I was an outsider, too. I always had been, but I had lacked the sense to see it. The *Maighstir* – with his fine new house of dressed stone and decorated plaster ceilings; his carpets on the floor; his silver teapot on the oak dresser – had never been on our side, except in idle talk. When it came to the bit, he would always take the part of the laird. I should have known that long ago.

He sensed, I think, something of the turmoil in my mind, for he put a hand on my shoulder, and said, 'Think on my words, boy. Talk it over with your father. He is a sensible man at heart. And if you should come to realize – as I think you will – that you are harbouring a wretched miscreant who should be cast out from your midst, you need only say the word to me and I will see that justice is done.'

I got up to go, but they would not let me away. Miss Nicolson hurried the kettle to the boil, while Himself laid off his chest about a Mr Cleveland, a poor man, the son of a pastor, who had once worked in a grocery store and taught in the Asylum for the Blind in the City of New York. Mr Grover Cleveland his name was, and he was trying now for the Presidency of the United States.

'That must be our aim in this country,' the *Maighstir* declared. 'Freedom of opportunity for all, such as our friends and kinsmen in the great republic enjoy.'

I was of a mind to say that they had fought a war to get their freedom, but I had done enough damage with my tongue. So I sang dumb.

But I did not sing dumb in the morning when I got a hold of Lachlann Ban outside the smithy. I drew him away from the crowd about the door, not saying a word until I had him on his own round the back, and there was the width of a double wall between us and any ears eager for a whisper of news. Not that I told him everything, mind; only what the *Maighstir* had said about the need to find the writer of the letter to the laird if we were not to be ruined altogether.

'He is wanting his name,' I said. 'He says he will see that justice is done.'

'Justice!' Lachlann Ban spat into a clump of thistles. 'What way can a poor cratur like Ailean Mor be brought to justice, and himself not wise? *Dhia*, the laird is in more danger every time he treads a steep stair than he is from the hand of Ailean Mor.'

'Do you reckon he wrote the letter?'

'Aye. Who else?'

'I just wondered.'

He shrugged. 'There may be others as far gone' – he tapped his head – 'who would be fit for the like o' that. No man in his senses, though.'

'The *Maighstir* says if we cast out the guilty one the laird will attend to our grievances.'

'Aye, he would maybe let us lift the drift timber from the shore,' Lachlann Ban said sarcastically, 'and the *Maighstir* would be in his glory telling what a great victory he had gained for us.'

I started to smile, but there was no smile on the face of Lachlann Ban. Indeed, I think I saw, in those flinty eyes of his, something of the barren weeks he had spent penned in jail. They were eyes that would never be deceived by empty words, not even from the lips of a preacher.

'The like of us do not win justice that easy, boy,' he said. 'If the laird had his way, he would shed the lot of us the way an old fox rids himself o' fleas – a piece o' dry wool in his mouth and into the loch tail first. When the water is up to muzzle, and all the fleas are in the wool, the fox lets it go, and that is him clear of his fleas. Well, that is the way of it wi' the laird. Near every year that passes sees us pushed closer to the shore, and more folk crowding in as their crofts are taken from them. Unless we fight back, the laird will clear us from the land as surely as the fox frees himself o' fleas.'

'I suppose.'

'No suppose about it,' he said sharply. 'The like o' the *Maighstir* is just windy talk over a kettle o' tea. Words are cheap, boy. If you could raise cattle on words every one of us would have beasts by the score. But land is not so easy come by. We will need to fight for our rights if we are to get space to live in this place. But not the *Maighstir*. All he is needing is fresh chalk, and the School Board will keep him well supplied wi' that.'

'Do you reckon it is right enough that the *Maighstir* has been feeding news to the factor?' I asked, eager to see what he would say when there was only myself to take in his words.

He shook his head. 'No, not him. He would be afraid o' –'

But I never heard what the *Maighstir* would be afraid of. Lachlann Ban was halted by a sudden cry of, 'The factor!' It came from Iain Beag. He was waving wildly at us

66

from the corner of the smithy, fairly hopping with excitement.

He was a terrible man for jokes, Iain Beag, and I was not believing him, not even when Lachlann Ban raced to his side. But I should have known he was not fooling. The clamorous voices around the smithy door had quietened to an uneasy murmur; Colla's ringing hammer was still; even the shouts of the boys – busy trying their strength at putting the stone – had ceased.

It was the factor, sure enough, and himself hardly ever in the place except for a rent collection, and that not due till November. He was riding along the path to the smithy, mounted on a grey garron, and moving at a lively trot. As he drew near, he slowed the pony to a walk; and, my word, the garron walked true and straight, swinging his long tail at every step, as a proud piper on the march will swing his kilt. He was a beauty of a beast, low and long with great strong loins and quarters, a black eel stripe along his back and a small star on his forehead.

There was not a sound as the factor approached the smithy, not the least murmur – only the ring of the garron's hoofs against the stone on the path, and the whispering wash of the surf on the distant shore. That, and the thud, thud, thud of my heart – loud as a drum beat in my ears.

Old Diarmad, a man near eighty, was the first to reach for his bonnet. He bared his long white hair to the breeze as the garron's small head drew level with his own. One after another, hands were raised and bonnets doffed – Coinneach the piper, Martainn, Padruig, my father, Eachunn Ruadh, Tomas the Elder – aye, and more, too numerous to mention; near a score of them. My own hand crept up and took the bonnet from my head. Only Colla never moved, his hands on his hips, his huge frame filling the door of the smithy; but his head was already bare. Colla, and one other – Lachlann Ban. And Lachlann Ban's bonnet stayed fast on his head.

The factor had halted his pony. 'You!' he said, jabbing his riding-crop at old Diarmad. 'What is your name? And why are the men loitering here when not a stone has been raised on the wall of the laird's park?'

Old Diarmad looked about him wildly. He was a timid old man, content to listen to the talk of others, contributing a high-pitched, giggling laugh now and then, but never saying much himself. I knew fine he was afraid – indeed, his face was very near as white as his beard – and I could sense his hope that the factor was speaking to someone at his back diminishing within him.

The factor transferred the crop to his left hand. For one terrible moment, I thought he was going to seize the *bodach* by his beard. But he only swung round in the saddle, and shouted: 'Answer me, you old fool! Answer!'

My father stepped forward, and himself a marked man, and one easy enough to spot seeing he lacked an arm. 'He has no English, sir,' he said. 'He is not understanding you.'

I had been afraid for my father, but I would take an oath upon the Holy Bible that the factor never noticed that the man before him had an empty sleeve, or heard a single word that was spoken, because at that moment he looked up and saw Lachlann Ban; Lachlann Ban with his bonnet still on his head. He nudged the garron forward, reining it to a stop so close to me that I could have reached out and put a hand over the beast's square muzzle. But it was not me he was interested in; it was Lachlann Ban, and himself standing straight at my shoulder.

The riding-crop was back in the factor's hand, tap, tap, tapping against his boot. 'Is this the respect you were taught in prison?' he said, not shouting any more, but the sneer in his voice plain for all to hear.

Lachlann Ban swept the bonnet off his head and gave him a quick bow. The bonnet was back on his head before he had straightened his back.

The factor's face took on the colour of Colla's when he

has been sweating over a roaring forge for hours at a stretch. His nostrils were flaring near as wide as the garron's. But still he did not shout.

'Remove your bonnet when I address you,' he said softly.

Lachlann Ban stood still.

The pony jerked its head up, eager to be off, and I saw the bit cut deep into the soft flesh of its mouth as the factor wrenched the beast's head down. The tap, tap, tap of the riding-crop against his boot quickened.

'Do you hear?' he said, a shrill edge to his voice, as if he was straining against the bit himself.

'I hear you.' Lachlann Ban took a step forward so that his chest was very near touching the factor's knee. 'And I am telling you that I have given you your place and I am not for doing more. You would like fine to see me on my knees, but I will stand straight before you or the laird or any other man in this place.'

There are some who say that when the factor raised his riding-crop he was not meaning to strike but only to tip the bonnet from Lachlann Ban's head. But that is lies, put out by those who cannot stomach the thought that one of their number is bolder than themselves. *I know*. I was by his side, and I am telling you the blow that was aimed at Lachlann Ban's head would have stretched him senseless if it had landed. What I will never know is how he moved so quick. He seized the leather crop as it was flashing down and held it fast. For what seemed to me like an eternity, but was no more than a second or two by the count of a clock, the pair of them disputed possession of the crop. Then the pony reared, Lachlann Ban released his grip, and the factor fell heavily to the ground.

He was slow in rising; that slow I was afraid he had done himself an injury. And he came at Lachlann Ban like a drunk man, shoulders swinging and legs spread wide. The riding-crop was still clutched in his fist. Lachlann Ban stood his ground, but he was the only one who did. Every one of us had drifted back like so much flotsam caught up in a strong ebb.

It happened that quick the most of them never saw the blow struck. Before Lachlann Ban could move, the factor slashed him across the face with his riding-crop. The flesh of his cheek opened like the belly of a salmon under a sharp knife, the blood spurting free, running down his neck and making a spreading dark stain on the grey home-spun of his ragged jacket. I heard him suck in a long, deep breath – and then he sprang.

Well, I am telling you, I have seen some fights in my day – bad ones, too, at the horse fairs – men, maddened by drink, battling without quarter until one was stretched senseless on the grass. But I have never seen any man strike with the fury of Lachlann Ban, and I will not grieve supposing I never see the like again.

His leap took the factor by surprise. The riding-crop was snatched from his hand and flung aside before he could make a move to defend himself. Even then, he moved too slow. Lachlann Ban's fists smashed into his face – once, twice, thrice – and he was not the only one who was bleeding now; there was blood spilling from the factor's nose, his mouth red with it.

It was David and Goliath, but what a David! A David with forearms on him thicker than those of many a man twice his size; whose big fists had been moulded to the toil of spade and *cas-chrom** since he was a boy at the school; whose back had been toughened under the weight of count-less creels of seaware, heavily laden creels, that had to be carted all the way from the shore up the steep cliff path to the croft; whose legs had been steeled on the gravelly scree of the circling hills and the long reaches of moorland bog. And it was a sham Goliath he faced; a Goliath whose big frame masked a body made soft by easy living, and a will

* Crooked spade; implement used as a hand plough.

grown brittle after years of command with the weight of the law at his back to make men shrink from the shadow of his frown and flee his anger.

All that was true enough, but it did not explain the terrible fury of Lachlann Ban's attack; a fury fit to storm the massed ranks of an army and pit flesh and blood against steel and shot.

Seeing the great bulk of the factor reeling under the blows of the smaller man; seeing him stagger and fall, rise to his feet and shake his head and charge like a maddened bull; seeing him halted by those flailing fists and beaten mercilessly to the ground; I knew fine it was more than a savage cut across the face that had made Lachlann Ban bent on destroying him entire.

It was the long years of oppression, too meekly borne, that was bursting out now in a blind fury of rage; a rage centred on the man who carried a wealth of harness on his pony's back that would have kept the like of us in food for a twelve-month; who was indifferent to the want he saw all around, but sharp to take affront at the sight of a bonnet not doffed in his presence. And, *Dhia*, I was afraid! Watching Lachlann Ban standing triumphant over him, ready to beat him down again if he should rise, I was afraid. The floodtide of that rage had been too long dammed. There was no knowing where it might sweep us all before it was spent.

It was my father who dragged Lachlann Ban away, and held him back, while the factor got to his knees, and slowly raised his head. He was done fighting, that was a sure thing. His breath was coming in sobbing gasps and the once sleek face was streaked with blood and dirt, frightening to behold now that the lineaments of power were stripped away.

He looked around for his pony. The garron was grazing quietly, no more than twenty yards from him. But it was twenty yards too much for the factor, and I believe we would have had to carry him to his mount if the grey had not answered his call.

The factor very near fell into the saddle, slumping forward like a loose-packed bag of meal. His forehead was grazed, the blood trickling slowly into his eyes. He wiped it away, and took a long look at my father and Lachlann Ban. Then he jerked the garron's head round, and was gone without a word.

For the first time, I realized that the three of us were the only ones there. The rest of them had melted away. Even big Colla had vanished. The smithy door was fast shut, and the tiny window was too caked with dirt to make out if there was a face at the back of it.

Lachlann Ban moved his jaw stiffly, and no wonder seeing the great gash in his left cheek, blood oozing thickly from the torn flesh. 'He is gone,' he said dully, like a sleeper waking at last from a long nightmare, not sure that the demons have left him.

My father was gazing at the circling hills, Beinn Edra heavy with cloud. I knew fine he was seeing beyond the hill, in his mind's eye, to the sheltered bay in the west and the long white house of the factor, the house that no man went near without first snatching the bonnet from his head. He gripped his empty right sleeve, crushing the useless cloth in his strong left hand; and when he took his eyes down from the hill I was not fancying the look in them. He stared at Lachlann Ban as if he was seeing him for the first time.

'Aye, the factor is gone,' he said slowly, 'but, wait you, the same fellow's tongue will not be idle once he reaches home. And the post office telegraph will not be slow in putting out word from him – word o' this day's work.' His eyes strayed to the hill again. 'Once the Sabbath is past,' he said, not looking at Lachlann Ban, 'this place will be crawling wi' the police, every one o' them bent on seizing the man who struck down the factor.'

Lachlann Ban jerked him round. He traced the long

gash in his cheek with a bloodied finger, and spat his contempt. 'The factor! Was it not the factor who did this on me? Aye, and near two-score standing by to witness the blow! And every one o' them wi' a tongue in his head, and able enough to use it in the court, supposing it comes to the bit.'

'Where are your two-score now?' my father said, glancing round at the deserted smithy. 'Good grief, they know fine what it would cost them to bear witness. And supposing they did? It would be as well for them to shout in the teeth of a winter gale for all the good it would do you.' He gripped Lachlann Ban by the shoulder, and shook him, like an impatient father trying to rouse a sleeping son. 'Make for the heather before the police come,' he said urgently, 'or it is you for the Calton Jail, and another year's harvest put by before you clap eyes on this place again.'

Chapter 6

They came in the dead of night, when every one of us was deep in slumber, bursting into the house that sudden the first I knew of their coming was a wild screech from my mother that roused me from sleep. Even then, I was of a mind to believe it was a nightmare that had taken hold of me – what with the long, black shadows cast by their lanterns; the shouted commands, as my father was ordered roughly from his bed; the shrill screeching of the *cailleach*, and the wails of little Seoras and Mairi; above all, the noise of the wind, no longer penned outside, but raging through the open door, driving the rain across the kitchen floor.

Seoras clung tight to me, sobbing, 'Is it bad men, Alasdair? Is it bad men?'

'*Ist*, boy,' I said, too startled, if the truth be told, to do more than grunt at him.

Peering out through a rent in the old blanket that shielded our box bed, I saw two of the policemen bring my father through from the other room. He was in his shirt and trousers; barefoot. Seeing him held fast by a monster of a policeman, another one, every bit as big, on his other side, and himself with only the one arm, it was in me to weep for him. Indeed, it was hard to keep back the tears seeing his bare feet – that naked and defenceless looking – beside the big, polished boots of his captors.

He was blinking against the light of their lanterns, and I saw now that there were another four of them in the kitchen, two of them blocking the door; the other two poking about as if the place belonged to them. One of them had the meal chest open. He was holding up his lantern and peering inside as if he expected to uncover a store of arms. The other fellow had found a tattered pamphlet of the Land Law Reform Association on the bench; that pleased with himself you would think it was treasure he had discovered.

The *cailleach* hovered near my father, a blanket drawn around her, her long hair hanging loose down her back. She was sobbing something terrible, and that started Seoras off worse than ever. He was clinging that tight to me I could not free myself to reach down the bed for my trousers.

'*Ist*, woman,' my father said, and then, speaking in English to the policeman who gripped his arm, 'What carry-on is this, dragging peaceful folk from their bed in the middle o' the night?'

'Save your breath for the sheriff, old 'un,' the policeman mocked him. 'You will be needing it before you are done.'

Until that moment – and it is the truth, as I am here – I had never thought of my father as an old man. Indeed, he was not old, not in the way that age is reckoned in this place, where the like of Fearghus Mor is fit for carrying a boll of meal on his back across miles of moor, and himself near eighty. But there is more to age than the count of years, and the policeman's words stripped from my eyes the kindly veil of kinship so that I looked upon my father for the first time not as *my* father but as a man.

Seeing him standing there, dwarfed by the policemen, his tousled hair and beard as grey as an old badger's, the marks on him of the years he had lived without the use of his right arm were plain to see. He had been twenty-five when he lost his arm fighting the Russians at Sebastopol, and that was near thirty years ago. Near thirty years not able to work the *cas-chrom* or wield a spade to thatch a roof or build a dyke or even tie his boots unaided. That was a weight to bear, I am telling you, the crippling of his manhood in the days of his youth; a burden far heavier than the weight of a boll of meal on the back of Fearghus Mor.

No wonder his face was seared with lines, like the face of an old man, and his shoulders had a weary droop to them. Watching from behind the thin blanket, I wished that I had the heart and strength of Lachlann Ban to enable me to leap from the bed and strike down the policeman who held him. Mind you, the way his back came up at the policeman's words, he was not needing assistance, my father.

'The sheriff?' he said, as cool as you please. 'Why should the like o' me be saving his breath for the sheriff?'

'Because you will be up before his lordship in the morning,' the policeman gloated. He tapped his breast pocket. 'I have a warrant to arrest you.'

My mother let out a shriek and put Mairi and Seoras into fresh fits of sobbing, but my father never gave her as much as a glance. 'On what charge?' he demanded.

'Inciting the lieges to violence,' the policeman said, the words sounding that awkward you would think he had learned them from a parrot. He jerked at my father's arm. 'Now, get on wi' you.'

My father held his ground. 'Amn't I to have the right o' boots on my feet?' he said. 'Or am I to tell the sheriff I was forced barefoot from my bed?'

There was plenty growling from the whole crowd of them at that, but they waited until he had pulled on his boots and the *cailleach* got his good Sabbath coat on his back. He said something to her that I did not catch; whatever it was, it started her wailing again. Then he looked at each of the policemen in turn; and themselves not making a move against him, held fast, it seemed, by his eyes. It was not sorry I was for him now, but proud. He held his head high, and he fairly curled his lip at them.

'Six o' you, eh?' he said. 'And all for a man wi' one arm! Well, well, I have seen the day when you would ha' been needed – every one o' you – before you had me out the door.'

They closed in on him, jostling him roughly across the earthen floor and out into the wind and the rain, and the darkness of the night. The last of the six stopped at the door. He was the one who had pocketed the pamphlet. He pulled aside the blanket from the wall bed, and peered in at me and Seoras, holding his lantern up to see the better. Seoras let out a frightened yell, and the policeman dropped the blanket. The door slammed behind him, muffling the noise of the wind.

'Are they away, the bad men, Alasdair?' Seoras said, his voice squeaking.

'Aye, they are away,' I said.

He started to cry. 'They have taken our Pappy, the bad men.'

'*Ist*, boy,' I said. 'Pappy will be back. He is away for a talk just.'

'They'll not let him back, I know fine they'll not let him back,' Seoras wailed.

'They will so. You mind Lachlann Ban was away. Lachlann Ban came back.'

'Was it the bad men took Lachlann Ban?'

'Aye. But they are not bad men – not all that bad.'

'Then why have they taken our Pappy?'

'For a talk just.'

'What will they talk about, Alasdair?'

'Ach, lots o' things, Seoras. You wouldn't be knowing.'

All the time I was trying to soothe Seoras, I had my ears strained to catch the least sound from outside. I was certain sure that the police would be going from house to house, and I thought I would hear a cry of alarm, or perhaps the sound of a struggle. But there was only the restless sough of the wind and the noisy beat of the rain on the door. I could hear our mother's voice in the other room, barking at Mairi to get back to bed. Seoras droned on, his questions never ending. I answered him without thinking, saying the first thing that came into my head, until his voice dwindled to a sleepy mumble, and his grip on my arm relaxed. He gave a sudden sigh and let go of my arm and rolled on to his back. His breathing was that heavy you would have thought it was an old man in bed along with me.

I waited a few minutes to make sure he was off, then I eased myself slowly out of bed. I felt for my trousers and pulled them on. As I was making for the door, a hand gripped my arm. It was my mother. She had been crouched down in the dark on the low stool by the black fire; a ring of damp peats that would keep smouldering until morning when they could be quickly fanned to life.

'Where are you away to?' she whispered sharply.

'To see where they are taking our father,' I said.

'Back to your bed, boy.'

'*Dhia*, no; not me.'

'Good grief, is it my own son that would take the Lord's name in vain and this the Sabbath Day?' she scolded, her voice shrilling. 'Back to your bed, boy. Have you no shame and your own father taken to the jail and it the Sabbath?'

'I am away to warn the others,' I said. 'Before the police reach over to them.'

'And land up in the jail along wi' your father, and put more shame on our name, fool that you are!'

'Well, I am going,' I said, 'and that is all about it.'

As I made to brush past her, she started to sob again. Quiet sobs they were, no louder than the flurry of angry whispers we had exchanged, but they halted me as no words could have done.

That is what I thought. But I was wrong. It was when she started to talk through her sobs that I was undone, because I had never expected to hear such talk from the *cailleach*. She carried on about how good it had been before the troubles started and our father had been snared by the false tongues of idlers who had no respect for their betters, and how happy we had all been in those days, the five of us secure together, and no word of strife. But now ruin had come, our father was taken from us, and our happiness at an end.

I was that dumbstruck I never said a word.

It is great altogether how you can live with a person all the days of your life, be flesh of their flesh, and yet have no more real awareness of their inner being than that of a birch bough stool or an old bench. That our mother could have been happy – *happy*; the *cailleach*! – had never crossed my mind – she who was for ever girning at us children and our father and his friends; she who was for ever casting up before us the great days she had known as the daughter of a *Ceistear*, and himself a respected man, even the factor walking along with the rest of the procession to the burial ground on the day of his funeral. My word, it was a shock to me, I am telling you, to learn that she had been happy.

'I will away back to bed,' I said, when she was done talking.

'Aye, that's it,' she said. And then: 'You are a good boy, Alasdair. The *Maighstir* thinks a lot of you. He was telling me.' She felt for my shoulder, and gave me a pat. I heard her go through to the other room, sniffing down her sobs.

I got back into bed right enough, taking care not to wake Seoras. But I kept my trousers on.

I have no idea how long I lay in bed willing the *cailleach* to go to sleep. It seemed to my tormented senses that I had lain there for hours listening to her tossing and turning and sighing to herself. Twice, I dozed off to sleep, each time awakening with a guilty start, half-expecting to see daylight coming in at the windows, but the house was still in darkness, and the same sounds still came from the other room as my mother stirred uneasily. For all my fears, I suppose I could not have closed my eyes for more than a minute or two. It was not in me to sleep. I had too much to do once I got clear of the house.

I thought the *cailleach* was going to be every bit as wakeful as myself, and then, when the house was suddenly deep in a silence that was near as thick as treacle, and I knew fine she must be sleeping at last, I was seized by a feeling that she was about to waken. I sat up in bed and started to count. I counted to five hundred before I made a move – and I could not have waited another moment supposing she had called upon me to stay where I was.

My jersey was at the foot of the bed. I pulled it on. My bare feet made no sound on the earthen floor. I eased the door open, and slipped outside, closing it gently at my back. There was not the least whisper of sound from within.

The rain had stopped but the wind was up, blowing strongly from the north-west, the chill of winter in the feel of it. The night was that dark I could not see my hand in front of me, and there was not a light to be seen from any quarter. Not that I was worrying. I was that well acquaint with the place I believe I could have found my way supposing I had been blinded. I had soon left our own croft and reached the path that wound around the back of the school and came out on the road above the bridge.

Once I was past the inn, I caught the full force of the wind as it swept in from the open shore. It was queer hurrying along in the dark before dawn – a dawn that would bring into being the Sabbath Day of rest and quiet – the whole place wrapped in sleep, the wind buffeting me like the boxing of unseen hands, and the angry surf roaring loud on the shore. The police must have been along this road long since with my father – and Lachlann Ban, too, if he had not been wise enough to keep clear of his house. Aye, and a full score more of them, for all I knew. I wondered what the time was. There was not the least glimmer of dawn. The eastern sky was black.

I never stopped to consider if what I was about to do was wise; all the way up the long, winding road to the pass I never once halted to wonder if I might not be walking into fresh trouble. It had come to me, lying in bed waiting for the *cailleach* to fall asleep, that there was only one way to free my father, and that was to seek out Miss Fiona and tell her the truth. My father had been arrested for making the people do violence – he, who had dragged Lachlann Ban off the factor when the same one was bent on striking him down for good and all! If I could gain the ear of Miss Fiona, and tell her the truth – and she had listened to me once before when there was less cause – I knew in my bones that she would get word to the laird, and that would be my father freed from the jail. And if it comes to the bit, I thought, I will tell her it was Seumas Crubach wrote the letter threatening to take her father's life, and tell her the kind of man he is, and then she will understand that the laird was safe enough, it was only the evil spite of a poor, twisted *truaghan* at work. If I could get to Fiona without the factor knowing, my father would never stand trial, I was certain sure of that. She had a straight eye on her, Fiona – the same eye as her father, the laird. All I had to do was seek her out, and if I got myself hidden among the trees at the back of the factor's house before daylight came, I should be able to get a sight of her before the day was far advanced.

A sudden, fierce shower came down as I was nearing the top of the pass, more hail than rain it was, striking bitter cold against my face. The wind raged through the narrow pass, the hail drumming like thunder on the rock. I half-turned my back on it, struggling along, bent near double, until I reached a cleft in the rock no wider than the body of a man. But I knew there was a cave at the back of it, and I squeezed inside thankful to gain a shelter from the stinging hail.

I was gasping for breath as I groped my way into the cave, and when I heard a sudden breath, that I could have sworn was not my own, I thought my ears were deceiving me. I heard it again; a quick intake of breath. I took a step back. But I was not quick enough. Hands seized me. Before I could cry out, or make a move to save myself, I was flung to the gound. I struck out wildly; felt my fist meet solid flesh. Then the weight of a body descended on mine, and the hands that had seized me were groping for my throat

Chapter 7

Feeling those hands at my throat, I must have cried out in alarm or shouted an angry swear or used my voice in some way to make myself known – although I was not aware of a single word issuing from my lips – because the very next moment the hands left my throat and seized my arms, and a great shout of glad laughter echoed round the cave. I was hauled to my feet and gripped tight in a bear hug, not a hug bent on crushing the life out of me but the warm clasp of friendship with which men of open heart salute old comrades. And Lachlann Ban's voice rang loud in my ears, exclaiming: 'Well, Alasdair! Well, Alasdair!' over and over again – and never, in all my days, was the sound of a familiar voice more welcome to me.

I started to laugh, such a feeling of relief flooding over me that once I had started I could not stop. I got weak laughing, if you can believe such a thing.

'*Dhia*, boy, I thought you were the police,' Lachlann Ban said, giving another great roar of a laugh. 'You gave me a rare fright, I am telling you. How did you know I was here?'

'I never knew,' I said, the laughter bubbling from me like steam from the lid of a pot that is hard on the boil. 'I was taking shelter just. It was me got the fright.'

'Where were you making for, and it the dead o' night?'

'The factor's house.' The words slipped out before I could stop them. I was thankful for the dark that he could not see my face.

'The factor's house?'

'Aye.'

What else could I say? It was too late now to change course.

'What was your idea, boy?'

I hesitated, only too well aware that it was no use trying to tell Lachlann Ban what I felt about Miss Fiona. How can you make known to a man a *feeling*; a feeling that had its roots not in what was said but in a look; the tone of a voice; the silences between words – words that were of no matter, having no part in the forging of the bond – so that without a meaningful word being spoken I knew fine that Fiona and I were as one in kindness and truth.

I could not tell Lachlann Ban the like of that.

'Well, what was your idea?' he repeated.

'They took my father,' I said, struggling to gain time so that I could think of something to say that would account for my actions without bringing the laird's daughter into it. 'Six o' them came for him and dragged him from his bed. Six great monsters o' policemen.'

'Aye, and another six came creeping in out o' the dark in search of me,' Lachlann Ban put in; no laughter in his voice now, the words fairly lashing out. 'And me on my back in bed! Good grief, on my back in bed I was, that thick in the head I was thinking they would never come near and it the Sabbath.'

'But how did you get clear o' them?' I said.

'They were wanting to put chains on me – wanting to shackle my wrists.'

He was silent all of a sudden, only the sound of his quickened breathing, and the noise of a drip of water somewhere at the back of the cave – *plop! plop! plop!* – like the sharp tap of a hammer it was, in the silence of the cave, that drip falling into a tiny pool.

'I was not having that, boy,' he said simply, as if no other explanation was needed.

'Aye, but how did you get clear?' I persisted.

'Ach, I put two o' them down. and the *cailleach* very near took the heads off the others wi' one swing o' that great iron cooking pot of hers. I made a dive for the door before they could get themselves sorted. It was the *cailleach* saved me. Without her I was done.'

'She is not slow,' I said, and, indeed she was not. There were not many in the place the equal of Lachlann Ban's widowed mother, herself as strong as any man, able to make a straight lift of a boll of meal from the ground to her shoulder.

'Aye, give me a score o' men wi' the same spirit on them and the police would never dare show face,' he said.

'Was it just my father they took, Lachlann?'

'Aye, himself just. I stalked them all the way up to the pass, thinking he might chance a leap for freedom when the horses were labouring slow on the hill, but there were that many along with him you would think it was a tiger they were guarding. I doubt he is in the cells by now, boy.'

'I suppose.'

He said, 'You never told me why you were making over to the factor's house.'

'You never gave me a chance to get a word in.'

'Well, on you go.'

'Ach, I was going to tell the truth,' I said, the words sounding that awkward in my ears I had to stop. 'About the *bodach*,' I added hurriedly. 'How he was not the man to be acting wild at all. I was going to tell the truth just.'

'To the factor?' He rushed on. 'What way would the factor ever heed the like o' you? Supposing you got near him – and I believe the servants would drive you from the door – he would laugh in your face. What were you thinking of at all?'

'Well, I was hoping to get word to the laird.'

'There is only one man has the ear o' the laird,' Lachlann Ban said bitterly, 'and that is the factor. And you may be sure the same one is not in the way o' feeding his master the truth. Not that the laird would be desperate keen to hear it, let me tell you. His kind would not sleep quiet o' nights supposing it was the truth they were after hearing.'

The drip of water went *plop! plop! plop!* I wondered if it ever stopped, or would it go on and on through all the years to come? And had it dripped through the raids of the Norsemen in the long ago when the people had fled with their cattle to the secret enclosure of green, high above the pass, and would it still be going *plop! plop! plop!* a hundred years from now when we were no more, the story of our fight for freedom as cold and dead as our bones. I shivered. It was that cold in the cave, my feet and hands were numb. I thought of Seoras sleeping snug in the warmth of our bed. What if the *cailleach* had wakened and found me gone? There would be a racket for sure; angry words – blows even. It was the Sabbath Day; the kirk morn and night and readings from the Book at home between times.

'What are we going to do?' I said, too dispirited for the moment to care.

'Plenty!' Lachlann Ban said fiercely. 'We are going to show them that we are not slaves to be trampled on at will. Listen to me, boy, and take heed of what I say.'

The first light of dawn was glowing red in the eastern sky as I came down from the pass. Seen across the wind-tossed waters of the Minch, the hills of Wester Ross looked like the beginning of a new world, as if the Lord had wrought anew in the darkness of the night and created those flaming peaks to point a way to the Promised Land of the prophets' dreams. The Promised Land, indeed! Well, well, it is great the daft ideas that can take a hold of you in the splendour of a Sabbath dawn. Some Promised Land, Wester Ross! The most of the people cleared from their homes long since, and shipped the length of Cape Breton and the far Carolinas; the glens and hills of their homeland turned into sheep walks and deer runs. My word, if everything I had heard about the place was true, it would take more than a touch of sun on the peaks of the high hills to turn Wester Ross into a Promised Land. At least, we still had a corner we could call our own, and we would not be driven from it that easy, not with men like Lachlann Ban to lead the struggle.

There was not a sound from within as I crept into our house. Seoras was lying on his back, his arms flung behind his head. I stood still, listening, letting my ears adjust to the rhythm of the sleeping house. From the other room, I could hear my mother's regular breathing. Mairi mumbled something in her sleep, and was quiet again. It was that peaceful sounding, the slow breathing of the sleepers, you would hardly credit that this was the house where our father had been torn from his bed no more than a few hours ago. I got angry thinking about it; wild at the terrible way that life goes on, no matter what happens, each one of us driven by time as a water-wheel is turned by a swift-flowing stream. Sleep was the great betrayer, I thought, listening to their untroubled breathing; sleep that puts a stop to all hurt, all anger, all remembrance of things past. But I was every bit as bad as the rest. No sooner was I stretched out in bed alongside Seoras than I, too, was sleeping, all thought of our father gone from me.

I got a hold of Iain Beag and Eachunn Ruadh at the kirk, and gave them Lachlann Ban's orders. That was easy done; just a whispered word of a meeting place and the time to be there. The hardest part of my task was the waiting – waiting for the evening service to come to an end; waiting for the crowd outside the porch of the kirk to disperse – and everyone, it seemed, bent on speaking well of our father to the *cailleach*; waiting for the supper to be eaten, and our mother make off to the byre to do the milking, so that I could slip out of the house unnoticed. And all the time I was waiting, I was wondering what would happen if Martainn Caogach did not believe my story.

He was short in the leg, Martainn Caogach, with a big belly on him, and the sort of ready laugh you would expect a proper dumpling of a man to have. But his laugh did not ring true when he looked at you because he had a terrible squint, and there was something about that squint that made you distrust his laugh, although he could not help his looks, poor man. He was a second cousin of my father, and the only man in the place who owned a boat of any size. Mind you, he was still paying the laird for the boat, and would be paying for her until the day he was carried to the burial ground, so my father said. He was the only man in the district to have taken advantage of the laird's offer to provide loans for the building of fishing boats, and if you think the rest of us were not wise letting go a chance like that, let me tell you there were conditions attached. One of them was that the catch must be sold to an agent of the laird. And everyone in our township said why should they be slaving to pay off the loan – at a big interest, you understand – and at the same time be putting more money into the laird's pocket, because the price his agent was giving for fish was well below what you could get elsewhere. And supposing the boat was lost in a storm, where would you be then with a burden of debt on your back, and no means of paying it off? But Martainn Caogach was not worrying about the like of that; all he wanted was a boat, and once he had got her he was in his glory.

I ran all the way from our house to his croft, and it more than half a mile to the west, on the other side of the river. When I reached his door, I was panting, and that made what I had to say seem all the more urgent.

'Your boat, Martainn,' I gasped. 'She must be taking water. She is away down in the stern.'

He was reading from the Book, holding it at arm's length close to the smoking oil lamp, his wife and four daughters lined up on the bench listening to him with bowed heads.

They had all looked up as I burst into the kitchen, Martainn the last to raise his head, first of all marking his place on the page with a stubby finger. Mind you, he was not slow once he heard me. He bent his head again, muttered a swift blessing, gave a loud, 'Amen', and closed the big Bible.

'Taking water?' he said, 'The *Sea Flower*? Never the day, boy!'

'Aye, right enough,' I said, desperation putting a sharp edge on my voice. 'It was still light when I was down the shore. I saw her plain as could be. She is listing something terrible.'

He shook his head, unbelieving. The *Sea Flower* was moored in the channel between the bay and a small off-shore island that acted as a breakwater to the northerly swell, and she had rode out many a bad gale at that anchorage.

'She must have sprung a leak,' I said. 'Another hour and that is her at the bottom, for sure.'

That got him to his feet, I am telling you. He made straight for the door, shrugging off the cries of his wife and daughters the way a bull shakes off a swarm of pestering flies. 'The boat will be right enough,' he called over his shoulder, 'but we will need to reach down and take a look at her.'

The *cailleach* caught my arm. 'It was good o' you to come quick wi' the news, Alasdair,' she said. 'Many a one would ha' waited until the boat was past saving they are that jealous of a man getting on in this place. Be sure and make back wi' Martainn and I'll have a bite o' food waiting on you.'

'Aye, surely,' I said, wondering, as I ran after Martainn Caogach, how I would ever face his wife again. There was one thing sure: she would wait a long time before either of the two of us was back for a bite.

*

Martainn Caogach was short in the leg, right enough, and the belly on him was that big you would wonder how he managed to stoop to tie his boots, but I have never seen a man take the treacherous path down the cliff to the shore at the speed he did, and at a time of night when the moon was not up. It was as much as I could do to keep close behind him, and him not seeming to think anything of it, tossing words back at me every foot of the way, saying how the *Sea Flower* was in better trim than any other boat of her size on the West Coast; her timbers that tight the thinnest-bladed knife would never find a way through; and telling of the terrible seas she had weathered. I thought he was boasting; too thick in the head to realize until later that it was himself he was puffing up, poor man, he was that afraid of losing his boat and him with a big debt owing to the laird.

When we got to the bottom of the cliff, he set off, faster than ever, across the stretch of marshy grassland to the shore. 'The dinghy,' he panted, wheezing hard. 'Beside the boathouse.'

He always kept his dinghy alongside the thatched boathouse where he stored his nets and gear, but he had got to the stage where he had to be saying something. For the first time, I began to realize what his boat meant to him. He would have traded his right arm for the *Sea Flower* and considered it a beauty of a bargain.

As we drew near the boathouse, Lachlann Ban stepped out from the low stone wall, Eachunn Ruadh and Iain Beag on either side of him. I heard Martainn Caogach give a grunt of dismay. He was not the man to fancy having his business nosed abroad, particularly if it was anything bad, for fear of people mocking him.

'Easy, Martainn,' Lachlann Ban said, hearing the wheezing. 'Your boat is safe enough.'

Martainn Caogach let out his eager bray of a laugh. 'Amn't I after telling the boy that,' he wheezed. 'But he kept on at me that much about her taking water, I came down to please him just.'

'It was me told him to say that, Martainn. It was the only way I could be sure o' getting you clear of the fire on the Sabbath.'

'You told him . . .' Martainn Caogach started. He stared out to sea, striving to pierce the darkness and make out the shape of the *Sea Flower*, 'You mean, you were having me on? She was not taking water at all?'

'Not her,' Lachlann Ban assured him. 'But it was the only way I could be sure of getting you clear o' the house.'

He was slow on the uptake, Martainn Caogach, but once he had got things sorted in his head he could move fast enough. I should have been ready for him, but I was taking my ease after the rush to the shore – grinning to myself in the dark, if the truth be told – and the first I knew of his anger was a terrible dunt on the side of the head that knocked me clean off my feet. Iain Beag helped me up, and it was a good job he had a grip on my arm because my head was fairly spinning.

Lachlann Ban had seized Martainn Caogach in a bear hug. 'Enough o' that,' he was barking at him, 'or you will finish up on your back in the boathouse, and we will make off wi' your boat whether you like it or not.'

'Make off wi' my boat?' he said stupidly.

'Aye. And we could ha' done it easy enough before now, but we were not wanting to tear the bottom out of her making into the harbour at Portree in the dark. You are the boy for that, Martainn. You could take her in blindfold.'

'Into Portree?' he said.

'Aye. We are collecting Alasdair Rob.'

Alasdair was my father's name, and Rob the name of his father. That is the way men are spoken of in this place.

'Alasdair Rob is in the jail,' Martainn Caogach said.

'Aye, and we are for lifting him out o' the jail. All you

have to do is put us ashore and lie off for a while until we make back with him.'

'Good grief, I daren't!' he exclaimed, backing away, the fright in his voice that strong you would think he was being asked to do murder. 'Supposing word reaches the laird and me with a big debt owing and Himself able to claim it back any time he takes the notion? That would be the end o' me.'

'It will be the end of us all supposing we sit quiet and make no move and let the factor put our people to the jail whenever *he* takes the notion,' Lachlann Ban said angrily.

'Aye, maybe so. But the like o' this carry-on makes the jail certain sure for the lot of us.'

'Ach – well, we will just need to take her ourselves,' Lachlann Ban said. 'Put out the dinghy, boys.'

They had already dragged the dinghy to the water's edge. A single heave had her floating. Eachunn Ruadh stepped aboard and fitted the oars into the rowlocks, while Iain Beag held the prow against the pull of the ebb tide.

'Wait!' Martainn Caogach cried, cluthing Lachlann Ban's shoulder. 'Wait!' He was near weeping, by the sound of him. 'There is not one o' you fit for the job, and fine you know it. You will put her aground. Run her up on the Black Rock. It is easy done, I am telling you.'

'Aye, easy done,' Lachlann Ban agreed. 'I mind your uncle from Sconser tearing the bottom out o' his boat on the Black Rock, and himself well acquaint with the harbour – and a good enough seaman by all accounts.'

'Give over,' Martainn Caogach pleaded; and then, his voice rising to a shrill pitch of anger; 'You are not wise, man. Whoever heard the like o' storming the jail? The police will get you for sure. The whole crowd o' you will land up in the cells along wi' Alasdair Rob.'

Lachlann Ban shook himself free. 'Well?' he demanded. 'Supposing the police get a hold o' the rest of us, you would be safe enough whatever. You could creep away in the dark, and no one any the wiser.'

Martainn Caogach gave the nearest sound to a groan that I had ever heard pass his lips. He stumbled into the dinghy. I got in after him, my head aching from the blow he had given me, and squatted down on my heels in the bows. Iain Beag and Lachlann Ban pushed her clear of the shore, and clambered aboard. Eachunn Ruadh bent his back to the oars, and the heavily laden dinghy nosed out slowly into the channel, shipping water as she met the choppy swell, the waves breaking raggedly as the north wind worked against the pull of the tide.

Nobody spoke on the way out to the *Sea Flower*. They were all taken up with their thoughts, not least Martainn Caogach. I knew fine the same one would be thinking he could scuttle off home once he had landed the rest of us in Portree. He was not to know that Lachlann Ban had thought of that, too, and laid his plans accordingly.

Chapter 8

It was a cruel stretch of coast south to Portree, mile upon mile of sheer cliff, a great rampart of rock, fissured here and there by the ceaseless pounding of the stormy Minch, cut by ravines where age-old rivers swept down from the hills, and mighty beyond belief in the way it rose stark from the sea against the night sky. Many a one had perished on this coast, from the Norsemen in their longboats to the brother of my father who had been swept on the rocks fishing for lobsters; and you had only to look up at that great, threatening wall of rock – and I am telling you it *was* threatening – to know fine it was eager to crush all who challenged its dominion, and the power of its willing hand-maiden, the sea. In truth, it was not a coast to be trifled with.

Mind you, Martainn Caogach knew what he was about, none better. And it was a wonder to me greater than any under the sun that a man like himself – a sly man, if ever there was one; quick to cloak his feelings with a laugh; slow to make known his mind; craven towards those in authority over him – could change altogether the moment he trod the deck of a boat and got the feel of a helm under his hand. There was no empty bray of a laugh from him then; no waiting on others to declare themselves before he said yea or nay; no fear of any kind at all.

Indeed, you had to hand it to Martainn Caogach – there was not his equal in the place when it came to navigating a boat off a bad coast. That was easy seen, supposing you ever had the chance of watching him at work, and it was in my mind long before he brought the *Sea Flower* round the towering headland that marked the entrance to Portree Bay from the north.

I was watching her prow creaming through the dark waters when a drenching shower of spray caught me unawares, coming that sudden it was like an unexpected slap in the face. I clutched a stay as she started to roll, her timbers groaning like a live thing, as she battled through the choppy swell caused by a northerly wind and the cross-tides at the entrance to the bay. With anyone else at the helm I would have been fearful of that great headland towering high above us, but Martainn Caogach never gave it a glance, nursing the *Sea Flower* round the point and into calmer waters with the ease of a man whose skill comes as natural as breathing.

I had my eyes strained for a sight of the Black Rock, but that long, jagged reef, the greater part of it under water, was past our starboard bow before I spotted its ugly black snout. I glanced back at Martainn Caogach, one hand resting lightly on the helm, as unconcerned as if he had all the wide Atlantic about him. He seemed to be taking more heed of Lachlann Ban, who was standing at his back, than the deadly reef we had just passed.

The riding lights of the fishing smacks at anchor winked bright in the darkness. We glided past them, dark as a ghost ship, the only sound the hum of the wind in the rigging, and the slap, slap of the sea against her high prow. I saw Lachlann Ban point to the curving bay beyond the main harbour. Martainn Caogach hissed a word to the other two, and they leaped to furl the sail. The *Sea Flower* went ahead on her way. Lachlann Ban ran nimbly past me. He lifted the anchor; stood poised with it, graceful as a figure from olden times carved in stone. When he dropped the anchor over the side, it went down with a splash that would have wakened the dead – or so it seemed to my anxious ears. I peered all around but there was no sign of life on the shore. The scudding moon lit the darkened houses for a moment, and slipped behind the clouds again. A light gleamed high on the hill. But it was too far away to concern us.

We came together in the stern. Iain Beag hauled in the dinghy as the *Sea Flower* swung slowly with the tide. She was no more than a cable's length off shore. As the masked moon glimmered through the clouds, I could see the dim outline of houses near the water's edge. The trees on the rounded headland that sheltered us from the main part of the harbour looked like giant sentinels poised ready to spring on an invader. Somewhere on the far side of the bay a dog howled, the mournful note of its call sounding clear across the water. I gave a start, but none of the others seemed to have noticed it. They all had their eyes on Lachlann Ban.

He had taken Martainn Caogach by the shoulder, and I knew fine by the way the same one shrank from his touch that he had guessed what was coming.

'Right, Martainn,' Lachlann Ban said softly. 'Into the dinghy wi' you.'

'Me?' Martainn Caogach exclaimed, in a hoarse whisper. '*Dhia*, no. I am staying wi' the boat.'

'You are rowing us ashore in the dinghy,' Lachlann Ban said, the harsh note of command in his voice making the whispered words more compelling than a shout. 'And there will be no making back to the *Sea Flower* the minute we are out o' sight. An oar makes a handy weapon, and we are taking them along wi' us. But you can stay safe wi' the dinghy, never fear.'

'I am for staying wi' the boat,' he protested.

'Alasdair will stay. On you go!'

There was no gainsaying his command; Martainn Caogach knew him too well for that. Muttering under his breath, he dropped over the side into the dinghy. Eachunn Ruadh and Iain Beag followed him swiftly.

Lachlann Ban said to me: 'I will make the cry of an owl when we reach the dinghy wi' your father. Start hauling in the anchor the minute you hear me. Right?'

'Right!' I said.

He punched me lightly on the shoulder, and slipped over the side into the dinghy. Martainn Caogach bent to the oars, and I was left alone on the deck of the *Sea Flower*.

I hung over the side watching the dinghy until it was swallowed in the darkness of the night. The moon had vanished, shut out by lowering clouds. I could hear the faint creak of the rowlocks, and then even that was gone, only the soft lap of the tide against the hull of the *Sea Flower* as she swung idly at anchor.

I have no idea how long I waited there, every creak of the boat's timbers bringing my head up in alarm. If the night was quiet before they had gone, it seemed to be full of mysterious noises now that they were out of my sight and hearing – the gurgling play of the tide; sudden moaning flurries as the wind gusted over the hill; harsh rasps as a stay adjusted to the movement of the boat – each one a separate pin-prick of fear, needing to be traced and discovered for what it was before I could rid myself of dread. And all the time I was expecting to hear the sudden shout of angry voices, the clatter of running feet; my eyes prepared to see the bright gleam of searching lanterns stabbing the darkness. I was that sick with apprehension.

When I heard a long, quavering *ooh-ooh-ooh*, I did not recognize it right off as the cry of an owl, and I stood rooted stupidly to the spot. It was only when I heard the unmistakable creak of rowlocks, the oars working fast judging by the racket they were making, that I moved. I dashed for the bows, tripped over some unseen obstacle, and measured my length on the deck, very near pitching over the low gunwale. I was up in a flash and on to the bows, clawing wildly at the anchor rope I was that desperate to raise it before the dinghy reached the boat.

Hand over hand, the weight of the anchor growing heavier at every pull, I hauled it up. At last, I had the dripping iron clear of the sea. Tearing aside the trailing weed, I got both hands to it and heaved it inboard. As I straightened up, panting after the heavy lift, I heard the dinghy scrape against the stern. I ran aft as Martainn Caogach rose from the seat of the dinghy and gripped the gunwale.

'Make haste, boy,' he wheezed. 'Lachlann Ban is wanting you.'

I had one leg over the side before I stopped. 'Wanting me?' I said. 'What for?'

'Your father,' he cried, not bothering to keep his voice low, the desperate note of urgency in it sounding only too plain. 'He is hurt – hurt bad.'

I dropped into the dinghy, and he clambered aboard the *Sea Flower*.

'Make straight for the shore,' he said, 'and be quick about it.'

I was not listening to him any more, I was that stricken with fear. Once I got a grip on the oars, I swung the dinghy round, and I am telling you I fairly put my back into it, rowing as I have never rowed before, heedless of the noise of the creaking rowlocks, pulling the dinghy through the water as fast as she could go. I never stopped to wonder why it was that they had not brought my father to me, and, if you would blame me for that, think on that there were oars in the dinghy, and I had it firmly in my mind that Lachlann Ban was keeping possession of the oars. And what with the long wait, stretching my nerves to near breaking point, and the sense of danger, and the desperation in the voice of Martainn Caogach, it was in me to believe that my father had been hurt that bad he was dying. And that was enough to make me heedless of caution.

As the dinghy grounded on the shore, I sprang out and

dragged her clear of the tide. At that moment, the moon escaped the clutch of the clouds and shone down on the bay, lighting the *Sea Flower* as she headed out towards the open sea under a full spread of sail. I gazed at her, my mind numb, hardly crediting Martainn Caogach's treachery, clown that I was, until she was no more than a moving blur in the distance. I was glad when the clouds snared the moon once more, and the bay was dark again, and my eyes were spared the sight of the consequences of my folly.

I must have stood there in a trance because I did not hear the swift rush of feet until they were almost on me – Lachlann Ban, my father – himself free again, and me miserable at the sight of his face, feeling I had betrayed him by my stupidity – Iain Beag and Eachunn Ruadh, each of them shouldering an oar. A flurry of urgent questions broke on my head.

'He is gone,' I said, and no words ever came harder to my tongue. 'He tricked me.'

'He must ha' got oars,' Lachlann Ban said, pointing to the set in the dinghy. 'I might ha' known he would lay hands on a pair about the shore.'

There was some cursing then, Martainn Caogach getting his character in words that would have shrivelled him to the ground if only he had been there to hear them. Not that Lachlann Ban joined in. He never said a word, too busy thinking out the next move to waste his breath on empty swears.

'Quick!' he said to Iain Beag and Eachunn Ruadh. 'Hide the oars you are carting, boys. Up the hill – in the trees.'

As they dashed off, he dragged the dinghy into the water, and waded out, towing it behind him, until he was up to his chest in the sea. I watched in amazement as he tossed one oar out then the other, and I thought he had taken leave of his senses when he upended the dinghy and pushed it out with the tide.

'That might keep them for a while,' he said, as he strode out of the sea, his sodden clothes clinging tight to his body. 'If they spot her, they will think we capsized, and are maybe drowned. Now, stick close to me, and not a word.'

He set off at a run, taking a track that followed the curve of the bay. It branched suddenly to the right, turning and twisting between houses and sheds, climbing steeply uphill all the way. We had come to the end of a narrow lane lined with high stone walls, a paved road branching off on either side and a dark alley, framed by high buildings, looming straight ahead, when Lachlann Ban stopped suddenly. He thrust out an arm to halt us, and flattened back against the wall.

I heard the quick clatter of heavy boots on paving stones; saw the gleam of moving lanterns at the top of the dark alley. A whistle shrilled somewhere to the left of us; an answering blast came from the right. We were trapped.

I had no idea where we were, somewhere near the big market square where the horse fairs were held, I think, but I could not be sure. Everything looked different in the dark. One thing I knew for sure, our only way of retreat was down to the sea, and there was no means of escape there.

'Over the wall,' Lachlann Ban whispered. 'Quick!'

He bent his back. Iain Beag was up in a flash, using his back as a springboard to gain the top of the wall. He sat astride, and hauled my father up. I went next, then Eachunn Ruadh. Lachlann Ban was the last one over. He dropped down as lightly as a cat, and hissed at us to follow him.

I never saw the like of that man for finding his way in the dark. He led us right across the yard to a long, low wooden hut without once blundering into the piles of stacked timber that were dotted about the place. The third window he tried was off the catch. He opened it slowly. One by one, we crawled inside.

The hut was full of the sweet, resiny smell of new wood; the floor thick with shavings.

'Rest your bones, boys,' Lachlann Ban said. 'We may be here for long enough.'

I felt something flat under my hands – a wooden box by the feel of it – and sat down on it. My legs were shaking, and my head had started to throb. There was a rustle of shavings as the rest of them stretched out on the floor.

My father said, 'You would ha' been better letting me be, boys. We will never get clear o' the place now, and it is the jail for the whole crowd o' you. I was not wanting that whatever.'

Lachlann Ban hissed at him to be quiet.

I put my hands flat on the smooth lid of the box, and leaned forward, listening hard. There was only the sound of quick breathing all around; the rustle of wood shavings as someone moved. Then it started – a shrill blasting of whistles; running feet close by; shouted orders. Another long blast on a whistle; a fist pounding a door. For one terrible moment, I thought it was the door of the hut we were in, then the knocking stopped as suddenly as it had begun. I could hear a low rumble of voices; somebody laughed; a deep, baying laugh. There was another long blast on a whistle; a loud cry of, 'This way.' A clatter of boots again. Then silence; an aching, fragile silence, swelling around us like a bubble about to burst. But no, it endured; sustained, I thought wildly, by the quick breaths of those around me. If they should stop breathing, it would explode – such was the foolish notion that came to me – in a deafening thunderclap of noise.

'They are away,' I said, my voice sounding like the voice of a stranger.

The door opened that softly, I never heard a sound. The spreading shaft of light was warning enough, but I was slow in heeding it. The rest of them had scrambled to their feet before I started up from the box.

Chapter 9

It was not a squad of police armed with pistols, as I had imagined at my first terror-stricken sight of that slowly opening door; it was one man, and himself bearing nothing more fearsome than a lantern. He closed the door as quietly as he had opened it, and advanced calmly across the floor, holding the lantern on high to survey us the better. It lit his own face, too; a strong, dark-bearded face, in keeping with the broad span of his shoulders and barrel-like chest. His bold, heavy-lidded eyes looked at each of us in turn, and found cause for amusement in what they saw, if I read them aright.

'Well, Lachlann,' he said, the shadow of a smile about his lips, 'you might ha' let me know you were after taking up quarters in my workshop.'

And I might have known that it was not blind chance that had led Lachlann Ban across the timber yard to this hut. He must have known that we would be assured of a welcome. Indeed, it was plain to see from the careless shrug he gave, and the manner in which he spoke, that these two were well acquaint with each other.

'It is not that easy giving notice, Somhairle,' he said, 'not when the police are hard on your heels.' Adding, as cool as you please, 'Are they away?'

The man called Somhairle nodded, his fingers busy working at his thick, black beard. 'Aye. I told them I seen you making for the shore. They were off like a pack o' hounds at the scent o' blood.'

'We heard a knocking.'

'That was them hammering on the door o' my neighbour's house. They are calling out the militia for to join in the hunt.'

'Ach, they would be as well wi' a crowd of old wives,' Lachlann Ban said scornfully.

'Maybe so. But the police will not rest until they have run you down, you may be sure o' that. It is not every day that a prisoner is plucked free in a raid on the cells, and the great Sheriff Ivory in the village at the time, himself not a score o' yards away' – he jerked his head to one side – 'in the hotel yonder.'

'Sheriff Ivory?' It was Lachlann Ban who spoke first, but the hated name was echoed by every one of them there.

'Aye, Sheriff Ivory. And you may be sure the police will be wanting the whole crowd o' you safe behind bars before his lordship wakens and gets wind o' the news.'

'When did he come?'

'Near midnight. Driving post-haste from Glendale. There is word o' rioting there.' He fingered his beard again; dark eyes inspecting the sober faces before him. 'Your factor was up seeing his lordship.'

'At the hotel?'

'Aye.'

'Any word o' what went on?'

'Old Padruig – him wi' the pin leg that has the cleaning o' the boots – has a fine listening post up above the games room; and it is the games room where the sheriff meets his cronies. There was talk, Padruig says, o' the factor being attacked and near killed.' He raised the lantern until its light was cast full on the face of Lachlann Ban. 'The factor is not the only one to ha' been in the wars, eh?'

It was the first time I had seen Lachlann Ban's face in a good light since his fight with the factor, and it was some sight, I am telling you, as if he had been torn by a monstrous claw. The proud flesh around the terrible cut was raw and weeping where it was not caked with blackened blood. Good grief, you could very near *feel* it throbbing just looking at it.

The big man lowered his upraised arm. I had the feeling he was wishing he had not exposed that ugly wound to the harsh light of the lantern, or let his tongue get the better of him. 'Well, well,' he said awkwardly, 'you will carry the mark o' that cut to the grave with you, Lachlann.'

Lachlann Ban said, 'What more did you hear?' his hand straying absently to his injured face.

'Talk,' Somhairle went on, 'o' the marines being brought in.'

'Ach, the Government would never allow the like o' that,' Lachlann Ban said quickly; a shade too quickly, I thought, as if he knew he must leap in at once before the dismay spread by those words had time to take root and sap the will of the others.

'For any favour,' the big man exclaimed, 'you have a queer idea o' the Government. What is the Government but friends o' the sheriff? Not friends o' you and me, boy – not friends o' the crofter – but friends o' William Ivory, son o' the late Lord Ivory, Sheriff of Inverness, Elgin and Nairn. And you know what they think o' you and your like, Lachlann? They think you are a crowd o' worthless, idle troublemakers, that ignorant you are no more than a jump ahead o' the heathen savage in Africa. Not allow the marines in? Man! Man! The same ones would be fair delighted to let them loose and drive the lot o' you into the heather.'

'Ach, well, we are not that easy driven,' Lachlann Ban declared. 'And the sooner we are in the heather tonight, the safer it is for us. We had best get moving.'

'Get moving? There is no moving for any o' you. The village is crawling wi' police.' He plucked at Lachlann Ban's sodden jersey. 'Away in the house wi' me, man, and dry yourself.' His dark eyes took in the rest of us. 'The wife will be out wi' a bite for you boys.'

'We are off now,' Lachlann Ban insisted. 'What way can we get clear o' the place once daylight comes?'

'Daylight or night, you will never hide the like o' that.' He reached out and took a hold of my father's empty sleeve. 'Many a one might slip by them but not a man wi' just the one arm. Any fool wi' half an eye would spot him right off.'

'We will need to chance it just.'

'And all the roads blocked? Patrols galore! The militia out! *Dhia*, no. Tell me, what way can you get by them?'

Lachlann Ban pondered, chewing at his nails. I wondered what he would say. Indeed, what *could* he say? He knew as well as the rest of us there was truth in the big man's words.

In the end, it was Somhairle who answered his own question. He snapped his fingers making a crack like the shot of a pistol, and swung round on Lachlann Ban, dark eyes fairly dancing. 'There is one way you can get him out o' the village,' he said, that delighted with himself at finding a solution to the problem he had to make a long pause and keep us all waiting until Lachlann Ban prompted him with a tense: 'Well?'

'In the old shepherd's box,' he said triumphantly, 'and it bound for Rigg at break o' day.'

I turned to follow his pointing finger, and I am telling no lie when I say I very near stopped breathing there and then. The box I had been taking my ease on in the dark – the old shepherd's box, as Somhairle called it – was not a box at all. It was a new-made coffin!

A thin drizzle of rain was drifting in from the sea, very near vanquishing the first feeble light of day, as we lined up behind the horse and cart in the alley outside Somhairle's yard. It was a gloomy enough day, by any reckoning, and the sight of the coffin in the back of the cart did not raise my spirits any. Not that it put Somhairle up or down.

He winked at me, as he went by, and gave the coffin a friendly pat, no more diffident about touching it than I would have been in laying hands on a bag of meal. He said something to the driver of the horse and cart, a little old man in a long, homespun coat and broad Kilmarnock bonnet, and got a grunt in reply that did not please him, for he fairly laid off his chest at the *bodach*, telling him to mind his instructions well, or it would be the worse for him if anything went amiss. The old man nodded, impatient to be off, judging by the way he kept shooting glances up and down the alley, and fiddling with the reins. And he was not the only one who was anxious to get moving. I was expecting to see a patrol of police and militia bear down on us at any moment, and I was thankful when Somhairle stepped back and waved the *bodach* on.

There were six of us walking in line, two abreast, behind the horse and cart. Eachunn Ruadh and a son of Somhairle led the little procession, then came Lachlann Ban and I – himself with his head well down in a high-collared black coat that shielded his injured face – and, last of all, Iain Beag and a nephew of the dead shepherd. I did not fancy the look of the nephew, a dour man with a mean eye on him. But Somhairle said he could be relied upon to keep his mouth shut, because he was getting the coffin on the cheap, and it was himself would have to pay for it seeing he was the one who would be coming in for whatever the old shepherd had left in the way of money.

The cart rumbled over the wet cobbles of the alley, and turned into the main street of the village. The shops were shuttered and dark; the whole village, it seemed, close wrapped in sleep, such was the air of brooding quiet all around. There was not a light to be seen; not a sound save the creak of the wheels of the cart, and the rattle of the horse's hoofs on the cobblestones.

We climbed the winding road high above the harbour

without meeting a single soul, and we were past the mill before Lachlann Ban nudged me, and whispered: 'A man coming. Don't be looking at him, boy. Keep your head down.'

The man had emerged from a big house some way back from the road. For all Lachlann Ban's warning, I could not resist glancing at him out of the corner of my eye. He had stopped by his gate, and was staring at us curiously. As the cart drew near, he doffed his hat and kept his head bowed until we were all past. Even then, I could not stop the quick racing of my heart, I was that nervous of us coming before the eyes of a stranger, and I would have looked back at him if Lachlann Ban had not hissed at me to keep my eyes in front.

On and on we went, at the same maddeningly slow pace – the measured, respectful pace of those who march behind their dead. The houses started to thin out as the open moorland came into view; soon they were at our back, the wide moor all around us, pitted by the black face of peat hags and the strange, grey outcroppings of rock. The road had changed now to a moorland track; a track that wound past lochs and across streams and rivers, a track that skirted high hills and clung to the face of sheer cliffs on its long, meandering way to our township in the far north. I did not think of our township and home – that was too far away. I thought instead of the handful of houses that was Rigg, no more than five miles ahead, huddled under the weeping clouds that hid the great shoulder of the Storr from view; and I wondered if we would ever reach Rigg safely with the coffin of the dead shepherd.

For the first time since we had left Somhairle's yard, I started to breathe freely. We were well clear of Portree now, and the only eyes that watched our progress were the blank, unheeding eyes of grazing cattle and sheep. The police and militia patrols Somhairle had spoken of must have grown tired of searching for us. Either that, or they had found the upturned dinghy, and taken it for granted that we had drowned trying to escape by sea.

The cart was toiling up a steep slope that wound round an outcrop of rock when I saw the driver cast a startled glance back at us. My foolish upsurge of hope was stricken dead at the sight of his face – the dull, pinched face of a man long drilled in the ways of obedience. I knew fine that the look on that face boded ill for us. Sure enough, as we topped the rise, and rounded the bend, I saw them – a group of police and militia officers. They were standing on a grassy hillock that commanded a view of the country for miles around, and I saw then that there was one civilian among them, a thin man in a knee-length, tight-fitting tweed coat, a hard hat on his head. He beckoned with his cane, and one of the policemen ran down to the track, calling on the driver to stop. The *bodach* reined in his horse, and we all came to a halt behind the cart.

'The fellow wi' the stick is Sheriff Ivory,' Lachlann Ban muttered out of the corner of his mouth.

I could hardly credit that I was seeing Sheriff Ivory in the flesh, and himself no more than thirty yards from me. Surely, that thin man in the tight-fitting coat could not be Sheriff Ivory – not Sheriff Ivory; surely, not *him*! There was nothing about him to show that here was the scourge of the crofters of Skye; nothing about that neat figure to make you believe that this was the man who had led the police in the Battle of The Braes; who had persecuted John Mac-Pherson, the Glendale Martyr; who had sworn to smite us down with a fist mailed in iron. It did not seem possible that it could be himself standing there, pointing with his cane; he, who had been the bogyman of my childhood – the bogyman of all the children in the place. Good grief, his name had never been off my mother's lips.

If you wander out on the moor, boy, Sheriff Ivory will get you!

You know what happens to bad boys? Sheriff Ivory

*takes them away in a big black bag, and that is the end o'
them!*

All that was long ago, but the memory of those days was
not easy banished. *Dhia*, he was not just a name to me,
Sheriff Ivory; he was the unseen eye that lurked in the
shadows; the terror that came in the dark of night; the
beating of the drum of doom. All my childhood fears came
back to mock my eyes and tell me that Sheriff Ivory could
not be a thin man in a tweed coat and a hard hat. But tweed
coat or no, I am telling no lie when I say that if he had
pointed his cane at me, and summoned me to his side, I
could not have moved an inch; no, not if my father's safety
had depended on it.

The policeman had reached the cart. 'Well, Ćalum,' he
said to the driver, 'what have you got there?'

The *bodach* looked back at us. For one moment of fear, I
thought he was about to say, 'The ones you are looking
for,' but he had only turned his head to spit in the lee of the
wind.

'Remains,' he said, wiping his mouth. 'Aonghas Caim-
beul, the old shepherd at Rigg. He went terrible sudden,
poor man.'

The policeman nodded, seemingly satisfied, but he had
to walk round the side of the cart and take a good squint at
the coffin. It was a blessing that Somhairle's son was at the
front of the procession, because the policeman knew him,
and he gave the rest of us no more than a brief glance, and
then not at our faces. It was as Somhairle had said, they
were on the look out for a man who was short of an arm.

'Right, Calum,' the policeman said. 'Away you go.'

The *bodach* brought the reins down over the horse's
rump, and we started forward again. Slowly – ah, so
slowly! – every measured step seeming an age without end,
we moved away from Sheriff Ivory and his men. I felt the
silence like the prick of a knife against the exposed skin of
my neck, expecting at any moment to hear a cry of, 'Stop!'

It never came, but I am telling you I was not done sweating until we had left Loch Fada behind, and climbed beyond Loch Leathan and started the downward run to Rigg.

We stopped in a sheltered cutting on the hill above Rigg, and freed my father from the coffin. The jokes were flying good style, everyone in great form now that we were well clear of the police, my father saying he was not sorry for the ones who had to be hauled a long way to the burial ground, it was that comfortable inside a coffin. Even the shepherd's nephew had to smile at that, and it would take a topper of a joke to bring a smile to the face of that silent man. We left him and Somhairle's son, and cut deep inland keeping up in the foothills until we reached the little township of Garros, hidden in a fold of the moor.

Domhnull Og, a first cousin of Lachlann Ban, stayed in Garros, and himself and his wife could not do enough for us. It was great, I am telling you, to rest on a bench again, and feel the heat of a good peat fire about your legs, warming the stiffness out of your bones. The wife gave us brimming bowls of broth, and there were scones and oatcakes galore, and a big dish of crowdie. I was finished first, and no wonder, seeing the questions the others had to answer, for everyone in the township had crowded into the kitchen, packing it out to the door, they were that eager to hear our news.

They told us that the police had been on the prowl in our township, and, as there was word that they were still about the place, we slept in Domhnull Og's barn. It was good to stretch out on a dry bed of straw, the warm, sweet breath of the cattle heavy on the air. I was asleep the moment I closed my eyes, too tired to take heed of the murmuring voices of the men.

It seemed to be no more than minutes later that I felt something tugging at my shoulder. I tried to shrug it off, but its grip tightened, jerking me roughly from my bed of straw. My father's voice reached me through a fog of sleep. 'Wake up, boy! Wake up! The police are coming!'

I struggled up out of the straw, trying to knuckle the sleep out of my eyes. The rest of them were on their feet; Domhnull Og at the door holding a lantern, along with a boy about my own age from the township of Maligar. He had run over the moor to warn us that the police had raided Maligar, and were searching the township house by house.

Coming out of the warm barn, the night air struck chill. A beauty of a moon hung low over Beinn Edra, the dark peak black against the night sky. The air was that crisp there must be a touch of frost about. I started to shiver.

Lachlann Ban took the lead, and he made straight for the hill, moving fast and climbing all the time. It was sweating I was now, not shivering, and I kept that sweat on me for he did not slacken his pace until we were high on the hill, and moving north along the ridge that divided the land like a giant backbone. He kept on until we reached Dun Dubh. There was one thing sure; no strangers would ever succeed in surprising us in this rocky fastness.

I could see pin-pricks of light moving far below, north of Maligar; more of them circling our township. Eachunn Ruadh pointed out the lights of a carriage, moving swiftly down the road from the pass.

'The police are on the prowl still,' Iain Beag said, voicing the thoughts of us all.

Eachunn Ruadh spat his contempt. 'Let them prowl. We are well clear o' them.'

'We are clear o' the cells,' my father said, his voice grim, 'but I doubt we are outlaws now.'

'Ach, well, we are not the first,' Lachlann Ban declared. 'Many a one in the Highlands was outlawed in olden days. Like MacGregor of Roro. You mind the song that was made about him?'

He looked up at the dark rocks all around, and down at

Loch Cleap, a moon-misted splash of silver far below; and I knew he was thinking about the outlaw of the song who had to take to the hills and turn winter into autumn and stormy spring into summer. I saw Lachlann Ban clear enough, his face sharp-etched in the light of the moon, and it was not grim he was, not at all, but smiling, like a man new-wakened to visions of glory.

'Like MacGregor of Roro,' he said proudly, 'we must make our bed in the crags.'

Chapter 10

It would be easy enough to make out that we had a terrible time of it, outlawed in the hills, and I dare say there would be plenty believing me supposing I painted a gloomy picture of desperate men being hunted like vermin. But that was not the way of it at all, not in the weeks before the landing at Uig. The police were on the prowl, right enough, hardly a day passing without a squad of them driving over the hill to patrol the croft lands far below, and strike fear into the heart of the womenfolk and the craven. But they never came near us, and we were not worrying supposing they did. We could have held more than the police at bay, for we had made our camp in the secret green place, high in the hills to the north of the pass, where we could watch the road without being seen. The hidden entrance to that strange table of green, in the heart of the towering rocks, was a boulder-strewn crevice shielded by a great pinnacle of rock, like a giant's needle; an entrance they could not have forced, even if they had found it. And we were joined there by a steady stream of young men from all the townships around the place, who came to us fearing arrest, so that by the end of the third week those of us gathered in the hill numbered a full score.

Mind you, we did not want for food, despite our numbers, because there were rabbits and hares in abundance, and we made forays down to the townships, under the cover of darkness, returning with supplies of meal, butter and tea, salt fish – and rumours! My word, there was always a fresh harvest of rumours to be garnered. One day, it was news that the marines had landed in Dunvegan, and put the people of Glendale from their homes at the point of the sword; another, that it was Vaternish where they had landed, some saying there was word that the people on the west side had seen the smoke of the burning homesteads darkening the sky.

There was plenty talk of that kind, but we were not believing a word of it, we were that certain the Government would recognize the justice of our cause once word reached them that we had taken to the hills. And if you think it was foolish of us to be expecting help from that quarter, I can only say that the weather was such no man could forbear to look upon the bright side. The sun, that had been lost to us all summer, had come into his own again in the late fall of the year, shining down day after day, and week after week, as if there was to be no word of winter – and bad omens, let me tell you, are not easy seen in a cloudless sky.

The days slid by as smooth as pebbles skimming the surface of a still loch, disappearing with as little trace. We tried our strength at putting the stone, and even my father took part in the hop, step and leap, so that it was possible to forget the grey in his beard and fancy him made young again. And there was many a hard-fought game of shinty on that smooth green turf, the wild shouts and the glad laughter resounding from the high hills – hills that had not witnessed such scenes since generations. But it was best of all at night, with a good fire going, the big tent, made of old sails on a frame of stout cabers, snug in the lee of the wind, and a tight circle gathered round the blazing peats. Then, there were stories and songs galore, and a feeling of kinship stronger than I can ever put into words; a feeling that those who dwell under the roof of a house in the lowlands can never know.

I believe it was something after the stamp of the summer shielings that I have heard the old men speak of when they were harping back to the great days of their youth before the hill pasture was taken from us – days when the whole township migrated to the uplands every May, along with their cattle and sheep and horses, taking a long picnic until the crops ripened and it was time to return to gather the harvest. Indeed, I came to look back upon the weeks I spent in the hills as the best time of my life – just as the old ones looked back upon the days of the shielings – because I was a fugitive from the humdrum duties of the daily life of the croft, as well as from the police.

In some ways, it was like a dream – a dream in which the sun was always shining, in which work and winter were forgotten, and the spirit soared free in the clear air of the high hills. There had to be an awakening, and I mind well the day it came. It was the eighteenth day of November; a Monday.

That was the Monday morning I met Domhnull the shepherd on the shoulder of the hill high above his bothy. I was looking for snares I had set, thinking I had the place to myself, and I was fairly startled when he came on me from behind.

'A good job for me you were not the police, Domhnull,' I said. Or the tacksman, I thought, although I never let on. 'Where did you spring from?'

He took his pipe out of his mouth, and spat. 'I was bent down putting a light to my pipe,' he said, pointing the stem at an outcrop of rock on the crest of the hill. 'If I had been a policeman, I could have taken you as easy as wink, boy.'

That was true enough, and I did not need him to tell me. I put on a laugh. 'Ach, the police are staying well clear of us. It is three days since we clapped eyes on them.'

'You will be seeing them soon enough, boy.'

'How?'

'Did you not hear the news?'

'What news?'

'About the marines.'

It was always the same with Domhnull, if he had news. He was not forthcoming at all. You had to work at him before he came out with what he knew, and even then it was slow in coming, as if every word was a bright shilling and himself a miser intent upon hoarding them for his old age.

'What about the marines?' I said.

'They reached Portree yesterday.'

'Ach, I have heard that tale before,' I scoffed. 'The marines were supposed to have come ashore at Dunvegan, and marched on Glendale. Then it was Vaternish. Portree now, is it? Good grief, it is yarns just. Lachlann Ban was saying the factor is after spreading them, hoping to give us a scare.'

He spat again. 'I had it from Seumas Crubach,' he said, not looking at me at all, his eyes busy scanning the hill.

'When it comes to spinning yarns, there is not the equal o' Seumas Crubach in the place,' I said, not caring supposing he was a first cousin of Domhnull.

'Seumas had it from Mata the pedlar. Mata left Portree on the Sabbath forenoon. He saw them.'

'What did he see?' I said, half-teasing him.

'A monster of a troopship. Her decks thick wi' blue-jackets and marines.'

'Away!'

'Aye. He even had the name of her – the *Assistance*. He is not slow, Mata, when it comes to the bit.'

There was no denying that. Mata the pedlar had been coming round the place since years, his goods slung in a pack on his back, and he had a great reputation for speaking the truth. They all said a single word from Mata was worth more than you would get from most folk supposing they had one hand clamped fast to a Bible and the whole day free for talk.

'And he said there was a gunboat at anchor along wi' her,' Domhnull went on. 'The *Forester* is the name o' the gunboat. And the steamer, *Lochiel*, was there, too. Mata says there is talk o' Sheriff Ivory being aboard the *Lochiel*.'

'Marines!' I said, too dumbfounded to take it all in at the first shot. 'A gunboat! Sheriff Ivory aboard the *Lochiel*!'

'Aye, and there is more, boy. Mata had word that the marines are to come ashore at Uig today. That is why he made straight for Seumas wi' the news. He reached down last night. I was speaking to the pair o' them.'

It made sense, unlike all the other tales I had heard about the marines. Mata the pedlar always stayed with Seumas Crubach whenever he was in the place, so he was bound to make straight for the tailor and give him the news. And if the marines really were aboard ship in Portree Bay, it would be easy enough for them to sail north and make a landing at Uig today. Indeed, it was the likeliest place of all for a landing, the village where the factor had his house. And Uig was the most sheltered anchorage in the west; a land-locked bay big enough to contain a fleet of vessels, and with the added advantage of a stretch of sandy beach where men could be ferried ashore in small boats. It all made sense, if our township was the target, for a short march over the hill from Uig would bring the marines down on us. Thinking of that banished all doubt from my mind.

'Where is Mata?' I said.

'Back the way he came as fast as his legs will take him. Fighting is bad for trade, says Mata, so he was for making off before the marines reach over.'

'You should ha' told Lachlann Ban.'

Domhnull gave an impatient jerk of his shoulders. 'And have him tell me I am not wise? You know fine Lachlann Ban would never listen to the like o' me.'

That was true enough, and the same one was not likely to accept the story at second hand from me, I thought. I would need more proof than the word of Seumas Crubach and Domhnull the shepherd before Lachlann Ban would be convinced that the marines were coming.

Domhnull misread the look on my face. 'If you are not believing me,' he said angrily, striding off towards his bothy and throwing the words back over his shoulder, 'reach over to Uig and see for yourself.'

It was not like Domhnull the shepherd to lose the head and stamp off in a rage, and the surprise I got at the sight of him storming down the hill to his bothy was such that I very near made straight back to our camp to tell Lachlann Ban what I had heard. But I soon shed that foolish notion. Supposing Domhnull was wild at me, that was no reason why I should lose the head, too. The shepherd was a first cousin of Seumas Crubach, right enough, but I knew the tailor far better than he did, and I was not for passing on any story of his without first making sure there was truth in it. Not that I decided, there and then, to go to Uig and see for myself; it was my feet that took command rather than my head. They led me across the hill road and deep into the waste of moor south of the main tributary of the Rha River. Once I had reached that far – and no eyes upon me other than those of a hovering hawk – it seemed as well to keep on and follow the river to the shores of Loch Snizort.

Lying in the dead bracken on the brow of the hill where it fell sheer to the bay far below, the River Rha tumbling down in a long fall, I was thankful that I had not rushed to Lachlann Ban with Domhnull's story. Never did a place look more peaceful than Uig, seen from the heights. The sun was at the meridian, blazing down from a clear blue sky, and the still waters of the bay mirrored the towering headlands. I could see the silver streak of Loch Snizort where it thrust inland; the slender chain of the Ascrib Islands far out in the loch; the long finger of Vaternish Point reaching for the open sea, and far across the sea the smoky blue hills of the Outer Isles. Of the marines and ships o' war there was not a sign – nor likely to be, I thought, looking down at the calm of that land-locked bay, the green strips of the arable land patterning the ground to the shore; a bright carpet close-stretched to the sea, peaceful, as only well-worked land can be.

Four fishing smacks were tied up alongside one another in the bay, the nearside boat looking the dead spit of the *Sea Flower*. She was higher in the stern than Martainn Caogach's boat, though. Likely, he would still be around Gairloch, for he had disappeared after the night of his treachery, and the word was that he had made over to Wester Ross.

Two women and a boy, all of them bowed under creels of peat, were moving slowly down the winding road from the hill, at the back of a heavily laden cart. Far below, I could see the tiny figures of people working at potatoes on the crofts. They were slow here; ours had been lifted long since. To my left, I could just make out the long roof of the factor's house. It stood between the two rivers, the Rha and the Conon – the rivers that had come together, on the night of the great flood seven years ago, and swept the laird's lodge away. Smoke was rising from three of the stacks of the house, drifting slowly upwards, smudging the bright blue of the sky. A dogcart left the inn on the south side of the bay. I watched it make down the road and cross the bridge over the Conon River, where it passed out of sight. It must have stopped at the factor's house, for it did not come into view along the road fronting the bay.

When I looked back at the bay, I could hardly believe my eyes. The bow of a great ship had appeared round the headland of Rhu Idrigil, close in to shore, and I knew at once she was the *Assistance*; knew it before she came full into view and I could see the scarlet tunics of the marines lining her decks. My word, Domhnull had told no lie – she was a monster of a ship, the biggest I had ever clapped eyes on. She seemed to fill the bay, as she steamed slowly forward.

Two sailors high up in the bows were taking soundings, their shouts carrying clear over the water. There was a harsh rattle as the anchor chain was paid out, and the great ship came to a stop, turning slowly with the tide.

I got to my knees, shading my eyes from the glare of the sun, as another ship rounded the headland, one I had seen many a time off Portree when I was up at the horse fairs. She was the mail steamer, *Lochiel*. There was a tight cluster of people up for'ard on her deck. I wondered if Sheriff Ivory was one of them.

The *Lochiel* dropped anchor on the shore side of *Assistance*, as yet another vessel came into sight round Rhu Idrigil. This must be the gunboat Domhnull had spoken of. There were signals passing between her and the *Assistance*, and she let go her anchor when she was midway between the troopship and the *Lochiel*.

Down on the shore, the crofters had stopped work and were gazing at the ships. Others had gathered at the doors of their cottages. A steam launch put off from the *Lochiel*, with a boat in tow, and headed for the shore. A bell clanged aboard the *Assistance*, sounding that clear it might have been struck within feet of me. There were small boats passing between the gunboat and the troopship; more marines mustering on her decks – hundreds of them, by the look of it. The bay that had been so calm and peaceful only minutes earlier was now all bustle and activity as the troops prepared to disembark.

I was that taken up with the scene I never heard the footsteps behind me. Before I could resist, I was flung forward on my face in the bracken, pinned down with knees pressed hard in my back. 'Got you!' a voice crowed, a voice I recognized right off as that of the laird's coachman. 'Throw dung at me, would ye? By the Lord, ah'll learn ye a lesson, boy!'

Chapter 11

'Scobie!'

The coachman's name was shouted from a distance, but I recognized that clear, assured voice at once, and so did he, for he relaxed his grip on my neck. He still had his knees pressed hard in the small of my back, but I was able to lift my face clear of the smothering bracken.

'Scobie!'

The voice was closer now, strong with anger, such anger as only those accustomed to obedience can command, making of a man's name a scourge with which to chastise him.

He took his knees off my back, and seized me by the collar of my jersey, jerking me roughly to my feet. For the first time since the fleet of ships had rounded Rhu Idrigil, I turned my back on the bay and looked inland. Miss Fiona was reining her pony to a stop on the other side of the low dry-stone wall that marked the boundary of the tacksman's grazing land. The coachman marched me across to her, never letting go of my jersey, even when we scrambled over the wall. It would have been easy enough to break free, but I was not going to run for it when she was there.

She had dismounted, and was holding her pony – a beauty of a chestnut mare, with a long silver mane and tail – by the bridle, and it was at Scobie she was looking, not me. Her cheeks were flushed, and I knew fine by the glint in those dark eyes that she was wild. I have said that the laird's daughter had a proud nose on her, and my word it was fairly hoisted high in the air as she gazed at her servant.

'Let him go, Scobie,' she said coldly.

'Begging your pardon, Miss Fiona,' he said, taking a fresh grip on my jersey, too stupid to see the danger signals and sing dumb, 'but ah got this rascal spying, and ah'm no for letting him awa'. The major'll be wanting a word wi' him, ah'm thinking, and maybe the police, forby.'

'Let him go,' she repeated, and then, as he made no move to obey: 'Do as I say, Scobie, or the general will hear of this when he comes tomorrow.'

He released his hold, muttering: 'The major'll no be pleased. The major telt me to keep an eye out for the like o' this trash nosing around.'

She said: 'That is all, Scobie. You may go now.'

He gave me a swift look of such concentrated venom it was all I could do not to take a step back. 'The major said ah was no to let you out o' ma sight, Miss Fiona,' he protested. 'I canna leave you, miss, wi' the like o' this yin.'

He shot me a look that showed plainer than words that he had no intention of moving, and planted his bandy legs wide, bristling defiance.

Well, I am telling you, it was an education watching the way she dealt with him – a man well up in years and as stubborn as only the mean-spirited can be – and herself not a day older than me, that was a sure thing. She turned those dark eyes on him, so like the eyes of her father, the laird, and looked down her long nose, and ordered him off. And, my word, he slunk away – unwilling, to be sure, but no more able to defy her bidding than a trained dog is capable of withstanding the command of his master.

I ran my fingers through the pony's thick-growing forelock. The mare pricked her small, sharp ears at me. 'She is a beauty,' I said. 'What do you call her?'

'Jess. What were you doing over here?'

I looked down at the still bay, glittering bright in the sun, the small boats busy about the big ships like flies at the flanks of browsing cattle.

'What were you doing?' she repeated.

'Watching,' I said.

She looked at me thoughtfully. 'Perhaps Scobie was right.'

'Wanting me brought before the factor?' I put in, made reckless by her cool stare. 'It would take more than the like o' him to haul me down to the factor.'

'Would it? He seemed to have you under control when I came along.'

'Aye, creeping up on me from behind before I had a chance to move. Once I was on my feet, I could have made off no bother, supposing it had suited me. It wouldn't be the first time I had left that fellow behind.'

'Would it not?'

'No. That night he was supposed to drive me home . . .' I stopped, afraid she would think I was trying to blacken the coachman in order to gain her sympathy.

'Well, what about it?'

'He put me off the coach in the middle o' the moor,' I rushed on, past caring about Scobie or anyone else, I was that wild at her superior tone, 'and I threw dung at him. He chased me, but he never got near.'

She frowned. 'Why didn't you report him to the factor?'

'Because I knew fine the factor would never listen to the like o' me.'

Her nose went up in the air. 'Scobie disobeyed orders – the general's orders. The general would have listened to you.'

'Ach, it did not put me up or down,' I said, aware all of a sudden where my talk was leading. 'He got me off the coach, right enough, but I paid him back in the end – and without running wi' tales to the laird.'

'Don't you think the laird had a right to know?'

'It was me and the coachman – nothing to do wi' the laird.'

There was a silence, an awkward silence that had me

searching my mind for a clue to the picture I had built up of her, a picture that bore no resemblance to the haughty stranger standing before me holding the bridle of the chestnut mare. I looked down at the bay. A steam launch was leaving the *Assistance*, towing a long string of boats, every one of them loaded with marines, their scarlet tunics and white forage caps gleaming bright against the blue of the loch. A detachment of police was ashore already, marching up the road to the inn. A Union Jack had been hoisted on the roof of the inn; it hung limp for want of a breeze of wind.

She said: 'You need not count them. I can tell you how many there are – three hundred Royal Marines and Royal Marine Artillery under Colonel Munro. And there is another gunboat coming tomorrow with more marines and seamen.'

I shook my head in wonder. 'Good grief, you would think there was a war on.'

'Well, isn't there?'

I looked at her in surprise – and whatever she expected from me it was not a look of surprise, I am telling you. The colour mounted in her cheeks, she was that angry; why, I knew not. It was not as if I had said something to annoy her. I kept a hold on my tongue, but that did not help any. Her dark eyes were fairly blazing with fury.

'Threats of murder!' she exploded. 'The factor attacked and lucky to escape with his life! Armed men roaming the hills! The blacksmith making spears for them! Isn't that war?'

'Making spears?' I said, that taken aback it was as much as I could do to splutter the words out. 'The blacksmith? Whatever for?'

'You should know,' she said coldly.

'Me?'

'Yes, you.'

'Why should I know?' I said, not realizing what she was

124

getting at, unable to think of a spear made by a blacksmith as a weapon of war, or that we – Lachlann Ban, my father, Iain Beag and the rest of us – could be regarded as warriors.

'Why do you think the marines have come?' she said, and then, not waiting for an answer, she was that eager to get it off her chest. 'But you will need more than spears to cow the marines.'

'Are you after believing yarns that Colla the smith is making spears for us?' I cried hoarsely, understanding dawning at last – and it was rage that made me choke and cough on the words, even more than the sore throat that had plagued me for days. 'That is lies just. Good grief, Colla the smith has not made a spear since years, and then only for lifting a salmon from the river. If you are after believing the like o' that, you would believe anything.'

'I suppose the factor was not attacked, then,' she said angrily. 'Is that what you would have me believe?'

'Aye, that is right enough.'

'That he was not attacked?'

I nodded.

She was that wild, I thought for a moment she was going to put her hand across my face. But she controlled herself, saying stiffly, 'I saw him. Covered in blood and only half conscious. The servants had to carry him into the house.'

'I saw him before there was a mark on him,' I said, not caring supposing she took it on the nose and turned her back on me before I was done. 'He struck a man with his riding-crop, and laid his face open to the bone. And you know for why? Because he wanted to humble the man into keeping his head bare, and him wi' the shame of a prison crop for all to see. The factor covered wi' blood! It was washed off long since, I don't doubt. But you should see the other man – the man who was struck first. He has got a mark he will carry all his days, and it is not bonny, I am telling you.'

She looked at me for a long time, not speaking, putting

125

me in mind of the laird the day he had gazed at me across the polished table in the factor's house, seeming to lay bare my soul. The barrier between us, that had seemed as solid as a dry-stone wall, was no longer there.

'Is that the truth?' she said.

'As I am before God,' I said, that hoarse my voice had become a whisper. 'And I will tell you more. That letter to your father – I knew all the time who made that up.'

'You knew?' she said, more hurt than anger in her eyes. 'And you never told?'

'Ach, it was all empty words,' I said, 'put together by a man whose mind is near as twisted as his back; a fellow full of spite, who would not know one end of a musket from the other. Supposing you saw him, dragging himself along wi' a stick, that bent over he would put you in mind of a crab, you would pity him. What way can you tell on a man like that, and himself not wise when it comes to the bit?'

A bugle call rang out below, sharp and clear. A long column of marines, four deep, was marching along the road to the inn. I felt her hand on my arm, and turned to face her.

'What are you going to do,' she said, 'now that the marines have come?'

I looked back at the bay, watching that long line of marching men, suddenly conscious that here, under my eyes, was the fist mailed in iron that Sheriff Ivory had boasted would be used to smite us down. The marines were taking the road to the inn, so it looked as if they were to be billeted there for the night, but it would not be long before they were marching in the opposite direction, along the road that wound over the hill to our township – that was a sure thing. And here was I, wasting time in idle talk with the daughter of the laird – talk that could not profit our cause however much it fed my vanity – when I should be racing back to tell the others what I had seen. The urge to be gone was so strong within me that I believe I would have rushed off there and then, if she had not laid a hand on my arm, and said, 'Well, what are you going to do?'

You need not think she was mocking me, because she was not. Indeed, there was such a depth of concern in her eyes you would have thought she was on our side, not theirs.

'That is the crowd you should be asking,' I said, pointing to the slowly moving scarlet column far below, my thoughts – and that was queer, mind you – on other things.

I was thinking of all the men of my blood – generations of them beyond number – who had tilled the land we fought to hold; men whose enemies on the Field of Culloden had worn coats of red. And such a feeling for the land came over me that I was aware of the pulse of life within it beating true with my own. I stood there, at one with the soil under my feet, feeling myself grow in strength, feeling the spirit of all my forebears – if you can believe such a thing – close-ranked at my back, uplifting me.

'If the marines have come to put us off our land,' I said – and it was my nose that was in the air now – 'they will need to bury us first, you may be sure o' that.'

She did not speak; did not say a word as I left her. I looked back from the crest of the first rise in the moor, a good half-mile away. She was still standing by the drystone wall, looking down to the bay below, the patient chestnut mare by her side.

Chapter 12

Long before darkness fell, word of the coming of the marines had been dispatched to all the townships around the place, and the people summoned to a meeting on the west side of the pass. It was Lachlann Ban's idea to call the gathering there, thinking it would give them courage to come together again in the place where they had shouted their defiance of the laird only a few short weeks ago.

They came, right enough, I will say that for them, and they came in their hundreds, a great multitude assembling on the high moor under the light of the moon. But it was different altogether from the last time. Then, there had been the wild music of the pipes to fire the blood; the loud cry of angry voices, swelling to a roar of sound terrible as the trumpet blast that sundered the walls of Jericho: now, there was a silence; a strange, brooding silence, putting me in mind of a Sabbath Communion held on the open hillside, when the people gather long before the start of the service, and are held quiet by a sense of the solemn occasion.

Even Seumas Crubach, perched high on the broad span of Colla the smith's shoulders, was without a word, although I believe it was the sheer size of the gathering that was responsible for the stilling of his tongue. He was gazing around as if he could not believe his eyes, and no wonder. In truth, I never saw the like of such a crowd. There were old men and young; men with beards as white as a minister's collar, and men with no more than the start of a smudge of whisker on their chin; men I knew well, and men I had never clapped eyes on before.

The young boys had been busy, ever since word of the meeting was put out, dragging driftwood up from the shore to make a bonfire. What with the load of timber they had got together, and the peats and heather and big fir they had gathered, there was a roarer of a fire going close by the flat table of rock that served as a platform. I wondered if the marines, from their base in Uig on the west side of the peninsula, would see the glare of the fire in the sky, and take it as an earnest of our determination to resist them.

The first man to mount the table of rock was an old *bodach* from the township below the hill road, a man well over the eighty mark, but active still, and one who had the name of being a great preacher. He spread his arms wide, the glare from the fire lighting his long, white beard and bathing the lean, brown face of him in a kind of radiance, so that he looked like a prophet of olden times about to bring the word to the faithful. Every head was bowed as he invoked a blessing, his voice deep and strong for all his weight of years. And then the voice of the precentor, Tomas the Elder, lifted clear and true above the multitude of bared heads, and all those present took up the words of the psalm, the music rising and falling like the wash of a mighty sea on a rock-fast shore. It was queer, I am telling you, hearing the words of that psalm swelling out over the moonlit moor, the jagged peaks of the hills black against the night sky, and the air thick with the sweet scent of burning heather.

Then it was Lachlann Ban's turn, and you would have thought he was making a prayer himself, he spoke that slow and solemn, reminding them that the coming of the marines had been promised long ago by Sheriff Ivory, who had called them rebels with arms in their hands, although their quarrel was with the laird, not the Government, and the only weapons they possessed were their bare fists. He did not know what lies Sheriff Ivory had told to get the Government to send marines to his aid, but they could be sure the same one would say it was being done in the name of the law.

He paused, surveying them all, seeking to win them to his side, I believe, by the strength of his will. And, my word, you could sense the strength in him as he stood there, not speaking, the long, raw scar on his cheek standing out something terrible in the glare of the fire. Seeing that ridge of puckered, livid flesh, you could believe he had been marked with a branding iron, like the slaves of olden days.

When he started speaking again, he was no longer subdued. 'You know fine what the law is,' he cried, his voice rising to a shout. 'It is the landlord's law – the law that is used to enrich the few and beggar the many. That is the law Sheriff Ivory is working for, and it is a poor rag of a law, let me tell you, that is needing a pack o' soldiers wi' guns to enforce it.

'But what can they do to us? They cannot use the bayonet on every man in the place. They cannot shoot us down like dogs for holding to the land that was ours since generations. They cannot crucify us for standing fast on our rights as free men. And if we stand fast, we are holding out for the rights of all free men, and you may be sure we will soon have a crowd at our back that will put Sheriff Ivory – aye, and the factor and the laird – to flight.'

There was no roar of approval at that, only a sullen muttering that was slow to ebb away as he spread his arms wide for silence.

'What do you see when you look around?' he cried. 'Every slope, every hollow, every flat seamed and furrowed where the *cas-chrom* has bit deep. And what has become o' the ground your forebears laboured over wi' such toil and sweat. It has been handed to the tacksman and his sheep. It is deep in heather and bracken where once there was ripening corn. Sheep crop the grass from the places where the homes o' the people stood. Our fathers were robbed o' land, and their fathers before them, and see what we are left with. Where the land is not rock it is heath, and where it is not heath it is bog – and not content wi' that the laird would drive us to the shore to live on limpets if he had his way of it.'

He drew a deep breath, and looked at them – looked at all those silent, withdrawn faces massed before him – and I knew he was well aware that they were not with him, conscious that if they were to be moved his way they would need to be coaxed along by guile, for they were afraid. He was wise enough to know that, Lachlann Ban, but it was not in him to try to mask the white-hot flame of his feeling. Indeed, I believe the sight of so many standing silent before him fanned that flame into more furious life. It was clear by the way he clenched his fists and held them on high that he saw himself as a scourge of the craven. And I felt their fear deep in my bones; fear of the military, it was – and fear of Lachlann Ban. In truth, they shrank from him as dumb beasts shrink from a naked flame.

'Good grief, the disease o' this place is poverty,' he thundered at them, 'and the only remedy is food. We cannot get food without land, and they would take the land from us. That is why the marines are here, to see to it that we are driven from the land. Well, I am telling you, without land there is no life here for you. No life at all. Is your only refuge to be the burial ground at the end o' the day, or are you going to stand like men for your rights? What is it to be?'

Someone in the very heart of that great throng shouted, 'You cannot stand against cold steel, man, and that is all about it.'

'There is no arguing wi' muskets,' another voice put in.

'Would you have us all destroyed?' a man shouted from the shadows at the back of the crowd, starting a deep-throated rumble of assent that gained in volume. 'What way can we face the winter if our homesteads are unroofed and our cattle put to the sword?'

The rumble of assent swelled to a roar; a hostile wave of sound that surged forward against that lone figure on the flat rock. It swept another man up on the rock beside him – Tomas the Elder. His face was a flaming red, and it was not a flush caused by the glow of the burning driftwood.

'This fellow will lead us to ruin just,' he screamed, pointing a quivering finger at Lachlann Ban, his voice breaking, such a rage he had on him. 'If he had not struck back at the factor, there would be none o' this – no word o' marines in the place, and guns being brought against us. He is not caring supposing they slaughter the whole crowd of us, he is that bent on downing the factor. Close your ears to his talk. Make back the way you came, and let each man keep to his own hearth. Only a fool would put so much as his nose out o' doors. Aye, and more – get down on your knees and pray forgiveness o' the Lord, for you have sinned in His sight, and we are all in His hands, even as it says in the Book.'

There was a silence at that. Then, the cry went up: 'Make no move out o' doors. Make no move.' And a great ripple of approval, like a long sigh of relief, ran through the multitude.

I saw some of those at the back stealing away into the shadows. They had heard enough, and were already creeping off to take shelter, Tomas the Elder's words strong in their minds, I would not wonder.

But Lachlann Ban was not done. He faced that vast multitude unflinching, knowing that the tide was strong against him, but determined as ever to rally them to his side.

'I will tell you how we can stand against the marines,' he declared, heedless of the angry murmurs of dissent. 'They have landed in Uig, and for why? Because they would not risk a landing here wi' the shore that exposed. That means they have got to march over the hill to reach us. Well, we can block the pass on them. Good grief, a handful o' men could hold the pass against an army. There are boulders galore in the crags. If we get them sorted above the pass, we can send them down the minute the marines come near, and there is no way through for them, then.'

Someone shouted, 'And them armed wi' muskets?'

'Are you afraid o' muskets?' Lachlann Ban jeered. 'And men among you who stood fast against the Russians at Balaclava? Aye, and many a one here wi' forebears that faced the English shot at Culloden! Can you not stand fast for the land that gave you birth and is all you have? I say we can hold the pass against all the marines in creation. If there are men among you, come forward and join me.'

Nobody moved. In all that great concourse, nobody moved. Not one; not a single soul. I could have wept, I am telling you.

And then, my father strode forward, his empty sleeve flapping loose by his side – and I went after him. We stood by the flat table of rock, and we were joined by Iain Beag and Eachunn Ruadh.

They came forward in ones and twos, but the movement our way was a pitiful trickle compared to the flood of men surging towards the pass. Now that Lachlann Ban had called upon them to show themselves, the meeting was breaking up.

Colla the smith lumbered forward, Seumas Crubach still perched on his shoulder, and I believe it was the whispering of the tailor in his ear that drove the big fellow to join us rather than any urge within himself. Mind you, Seumas Crubach was not whispering now, not him. His deep, deep voice boomed out at the backs of those in retreat, mocking them for cowards that they could use the strength of their legs to flee and not be weakened by shame at the sight of himself standing fast.

I felt dizzy, sweating the one moment with the heat of the fire on my back, and shivering the next as the chill night air struck through my thin jersey. I blinked the dizziness away, and counted those of us standing by the roof – twelve, not taking the tailor into account, and you could not reckon him as a whole man.

Lachlann Ban was beside me. He put a hand on my shoulder. 'You are shivering, boy,' he said.

'Good grief, Lachlann,' I exclaimed, 'there are not many of us. Twelve just.'

'Ach, well, the Lord Himself had no more for a start.' He squeezed my shoulder. 'We will halt them, boy, never fear.'

Colla the smith had lowered Seumas Crubach to the ground. Lachlann Ban moved across to them, and laid a big hand on the tailor's thin shoulder. 'It was good o' you to come forward, Seumas,' he said quietly, 'but we cannot make use o' you in the hill, and that is the plain truth, as I am here. The track above the pass would take the heart out o' many a man twice your size.'

Lachlann Ban had put it well, in words that could do no hurt, but you never could tell with Seumas Crubach, and it would not have surprised me if he had taken it on the nose. He was a terrible man for flying into a rage, and giving you dogs' abuse, if he got the least notion that you were making out that he was not as other men. But all he said was: 'Ach, Colla will give me a lift, no bother. Colla has the strength for the two of us, and more besides.'

'Colla will need all his strength for heaving boulders,' Lachlann Ban said. 'But I doubt he will need to give you a lift down home, Seumas.'

The tailor pushed himself up on his stick, one shoulder higher than the other as he tried to conceal his crooked back. '*Dhia*, no,' he said angrily, 'I am not for a lift down home at all.' He looked up at the giant figure of the smith. 'On you go wi' the rest, Colla. I will reach over to the bothy o' my cousin, Domhnull. Maybe I am not able for moving boulders, but I will stay where I can give the marines the length o' my tongue the minute they come into sight.' His thin, sharp face broke into a rare smile, as he squinted up at Lachlann Ban. 'I have a tongue, Lachlann, and I will use it on them before I am done, you may be sure o' that.'

I had never much fancied Seumas Crubach, thinking him a mean-natured and spiteful man, not taking into account, I admit, the way he was caged in a twisted body that held him trapped worse than a prisoner in chains. But I looked at him with a new respect, as he dragged himself off towards the shepherd's bothy, watching every stabbing move of the stick, each queer, shuffling, crablike step he took, with a feeling of shame that it was the first time I had been aware of the effort of will it must cost him to put one foot after the other. There was not one of us there, I am sure, who did not wish that the rest of the men in the place had the half of his spirit.

'Well, he is not slow, I am telling you,' Iain Beag said. He chuckled. 'The marines are in for a fright when they get the length o' Domhnull's bothy and clap eyes on Seumas. They will be after hearing swears that will put their ears on fire just.'

Colla the smith said, 'Cripple and all, you have got to hand it to him. He has a right heart on him, that one.'

Lachlann Ban was gazing into the red heart of the dying fire as if he was seeing pictures there. He squared his shoulders, and looked at each one of his little group of followers in turn. 'There is work to be done,' he said grimly, 'if we are to be ready for the marines, and the same ones may be here before the dawn is long past.'

Something moved in the shadows at the entrance to the pass. I stared in amazement as a girl came slowly forward, timid as a wild thing approaching the camp of men. It was my sister, Mairi, and it was not the light of the moon that made her face look as pale as the flesh of a skinned rabbit.

'What is it, girl?' our father said, catching her by the arm.

She stared at him, wide-eyed, and slowly shifted her gaze to me. 'The *Maighstir* is waiting at the house,' she whispered. 'He says he has a message for Alasdair – a terrible important message.'

Chapter 13

We ran most of the way home, Mairi and I, and it was not herself who flagged first, but me. Before we had covered half the distance, I was panting like an old dog whereas Mairi was breathing that easy you would not know she had been running at all. Mind you, I could have left her far behind, if I had been in my usual trim, but the sore throat that had plagued me for so long seemed to have put a chill deep in my bones, stiffening my joints and sapping my strength. It was pride alone that kept me going, but even pride had to succumb to the fit of coughing that seized me as I toiled behind Mairi up the track that wound round the back of the school to our croft. I stopped, bent double, coughing and retching something terrible.

Mairi came back, and waited for me. 'If the *cailleach* hears you making a racket like that,' she said, 'it is you for your bed.'

'No bed for me, girl,' I gasped, scrubbing at my streaming eyes with the back of my hand. 'I have work to do tonight yet.'

I was taking no chances, though, and I walked the rest of the way home, content to let Mairi skip on ahead. I was determined not to be seized by another fit of coughing as I came in the door, and have the *Maighstir* on at me, as well as our mother.

I ducked under the low stone lintel and hurried into the kitchen, blinking the thick peat reek out of my eyes. Mairi was perched on the edge of the bench, little Seoras beside her. The pair of them were looking that fearful, it came to me in a flash that the *Maighstir* must have left word of his message with our mother, and they knew it to be bad. At any rate, there was no sign of him. He was not in the kitchen.

The *cailleach* got up from the low birch bough stool by the fire. She had failed something awful in the weeks my father and I had been away in the hill. Her face had become strangely shrunken and pinched, the skin drawn tight over the bones, making of her countenance a mask. In some ways, she had taken on a look of her father, the old *Ceistear*. His eyes had always been deep-sunk and darkly shadowed, seeming to look through you to some black pit that only he could fathom. And that was the way she was looking at me now, with the same haunted eyes.

'Where is the *Maighstir*?' I said.

She brushed past me, and closed the door, and stood with her back to it. 'In his bed, if he is wise. Where you should be.' She put a hand on my forehead. 'You are soaking wi' sweat, boy.'

'Ach, I was running. What about the *Maighstir's* message? What news had he for me?'

'There was no message.' She drew a long, sobbing breath, but it was not weeping she was at, not her; it was rage that made her tremble so. And her rage was directed at me, the words beating about my ears in a shrill barrage that very near put me dizzy.

'You think you are having the great times of it, I know fine, trailing the hill along wi' your father, the pair o' you no better than footloose tinkers, but I will put a stop to that carry-on. Your father is off his head altogether, but I am not for seeing any son o' mine go the same road. Think o' the disgrace of it, boy, when soldiers are needing sent to the place because the laird is that vexed wi' us – and your father bent on defying them, fool that he is. Are you wanting to be shot dead, the pair o' you? What way will that bring food to the hungry, tell me that, if you can?

You are not wise, the lot o' you. That Lachlann Ban is after making you as bad as himself. Well, I am not having it, see. You will not stir out o' the house this night – no, nor tomorrow either. I am putting a tether on you, boy. The days o' your roaming are done, as long as I am mistress here.'

I was that taken aback, I stood there in a sort of stunned silence, fairly seething with anger and dismay. Good grief, I had not expected my own mother to play me false!

'Tomas the Elder has been on at you,' I said hoarsely. 'A fine one to be listening to, Tomas! A right rag of a man, I am telling you, too craven to stand wi' the rest of us.'

'Ist!' she cried. 'Not another word!' Her lips trembled. 'The nerve o' you, boy, making lies on a good man, and himself an elder!'

'Making lies, is it?' I shouted, near beside myself with rage. 'It was yourself was making lies, and fine you know it.' I whirled round on Mairi. 'You knew it was lies, too. I will sort you, girl that is a sure thing.'

As I lifted my hand to her, she darted behind the table. The *cailleach* caught me by the jersey, and dragged me back. 'Enough, boy,' she shrilled, 'or I will take a stick to your back. It was myself told Mairi what to do, right enough, and she knew fine what would happen to her supposing she landed home without you. And Mairi is not the only one who will do my bidding. From this night on, it is me telling you what to do, and you had best get that into your head, thick an' all as it is.'

'I am not needing any telling from you,' I blustered, gazing about me like a trapped animal that knows it is cornered but lacks the courage to make a direct dash for freedom.

Seoras had started to cry. Mairi was crouched behind the table, very near weeping herself. I glared at her, that wild I would have made her ears ring if only I could have got a hand to her. Our mother was the only calm one there. She knew well enough that the strongest tethers were not made of rope or chain.

I took a step towards her. 'I am away to our father, and that is all about it,' I said.

'Never the day,' she declared, moving back and blocking the door.

'Out o' the way,' I insisted. 'I am going, I tell you.'

'There is only one way you will go, boy,' she said fiercely, 'supposing I have to stand before this door the long night through, and that is by striking your mother down. Are you fit for the like o' that, eh? Are you that far gone you would use your fists on your own mother?'

I raged at her, but to no avail. I pleaded with her, but she would not budge. In the end, I went and sat on the bench, heedless of Seoras's frightened sobs, I was that busy plotting how to get by her. There was one thing sure, the moment she moved from the door that was me out of the house.

But she did not move, not her. She ordered Mairi to take her the stool, and squatted down on it with her back against the door. And she gave no sign of tiring of her stance. Indeed, now that she had got me safely penned indoors, she was in her glory, as busy giving orders as the captain of a ship. Seoras was to stop weeping and get to his bed, and Mairi was to make up the fire with fresh peats.

'And make a bowl o' brose for that boy,' she said, giving me a glowering look that put me in mind, once more, of her father, the *Ceistear*. 'He is needing a bite by the look o' him. And put dry tea in the pot, girl. We could all be doing with a cup o' tea.'

'I am not wanting tea,' I said, 'nor brose either.' Neither I was. My head seemed to be on fire, and my throat was that sore it was as much as I could do to swallow my own saliva.

'Sulking won't help you,' she crowed. 'You are here to stay, and that is all about it.'

I watched in silence, as she and Mairi took tea, Mairi keeping well away from me as she buttered a piece of girdle scone. The *cailleach* never stirred from the stool. Mairi went off to bed when she had taken her piece, but our mother stayed by the door.

I tried once more to get her to change her mind, using all the arguments I could think of, and keeping on at her for long enough, but it was no use. In despair, I got into bed alongside Seoras. Mind you, I did not take my clothes off, for I knew she would hide my trousers on me if she got the chance, so I lay in bed fully dressed, ready to make off if she should ever think that I was sleeping and go into the other room.

Seoras, the clown, started whispering to me. I hissed at him to be quiet, and get off to sleep, my eyes fixed on a tear in the blanket that hung across the opening of the wall bed; a tear that gave me a view of the door.

Well, I am telling you, she had some patience, the *cailleach*. The fire dwindled to a crumbling heap of red ash, but she never moved from her place by the door. Seoras had been sleeping for hours – or so it seemed to me – when she got up and crossed to our bed, and slowly lifted the blanket curtain. I kept my eyes tight shut, breathing deep and slow. She muttered something to herself. I felt a draught on my sweating face as the curtain fell back. Her boots squeaked as she moved away. When I opened my eyes, and peered through the tear in the curtain, she was back on the stool by the door.

It was that hot in bed, I was soaked in sweat, and my eyes were smarting something terrible. It was as if I had grit in them. It was as well for me to shut my eyes, anyway. There was no more than a glimmer of light in the room, the most of it coming from the red ashes of the fire. If she moved, I would hear the squeak of her boots.

I can remember opening my eyes, and seeing the oil lamp flicker and go out. I peered at my mother, seeing her dimly in the faint glow cast by the dying fire. She was leaning back against the door, her hands clasped in her lap. When I closed my eyes again, I knew fine I was drifting off to sleep, but I was too weary and sick at heart to fight against it.

I had my back against a high wall at the end of a long, brightly-lit alley. A man was coming towards me; a monster of a man in a brilliant scarlet tunic, carrying a riding-crop with a bayonet fixed on the end of it. I got the shock of my life when I saw that the man had the face of the factor. I tried to run, but I was held fast to the wall, unable to move a muscle, although I was pouring with sweat, so great was the effort I made to escape him. On and on he came, grinning evilly at me, his face growing bigger with every step he took, until it loomed above me like a monstrous full moon. 'Ah'll learn ye a lesson, boy,' he growled, and the voice that issued from his lips was the voice of the laird's coachman. The dull steel of the bayonet glinted in the light as he raised the riding-crop above his head, but before he could bring it down the brightly-lit alley was suddenly plunged in darkness.

I awoke to find myself sitting up in bed, sobbing for breath, the sweat running free down my face. The steady breathing of little Seoras slowed the quick beat of my heart, and helped clear my mind of the evil shadows of the nightmare. I pulled the curtain aside, and got out of bed. The faint, grey light of early dawn was starting to seep into the room, wresting the contents of the kitchen – the rough-hewn table, the bench, the meal chest – away from the hub of night. I stumbled towards the door, still half-dazed with sleep.

I never saw the *cailleach* at all, for her black boots, black stockings, and long black skirt merged with the shadows, and I tripped over her outstretched legs. She must have been sleeping, for she gave a cry of alarm. But she was not slow in springing up from the low stool and seizing my wrists.

'Back to your bed, boy,' she cried fiercely. 'There is to be no prowling while I am here.'

'Let go o' me,' I protested, maddened to find her still on guard. 'I am not a dog to be chained to your heel for the rest o' my life.'

I twisted my wrists free of her hold, and she struck out wildly at me, catching me a blow flush on the nose. I staggered back, feeling the blood spouting from my nose. It gushed forth, like a fountain, spattering down on the earthen floor between us. The tears that came to my eyes were not of pain or rage; they were tears of self-pity that she could so ill use me.

The stool had been kicked aside in our brief struggle. The *cailleach* dragged the door open, to enable her to see the better. I bent my head forward to stop the stream of blood soaking my jersey and trousers.

'Put your head back, boy,' she pleaded, her mouth working, she was that vexed with herself for having struck the blow, she who could never stand the sight of blood. 'Wait you, Alasdair. I will get a cloth and water.'

She hurried past me to the corner of the room where the water pail was kept.

The moment her back was turned, I was out the open door, bounding away like a hare into the grey mist of the early morning, heedless of her angry cries at my back. I did not stop running until I came to the bridge over the river.

Once I had bathed my face in the icy water of the river, and lain back on the wet bank until the bleeding stopped, I lost no time in making for the hill. The peaks were hidden in mist, smoky white clouds of it eddying about the foot-hills, lifting slowly as the dawn calm was broken by the first breeze of wind of the day.

I should have kept to the road, but I was that anxious to gain the pass before the coming of full daylight that I took

143

a short-cut, following the sheep tracks that wound up the steep face of the hill. Before long, the trailing clouds of mist were swirling all around me, and I had entered a wet, silent world, close-shuttered the one moment, and open the next, as the rising wind lifted the heavy white vapour to higher ground, and revealed the way ahead.

I stopped for a moment, toeing aside the empty skin of a rabbit and a mole – refuse from the nest of a hawk – and I heard the unmistakable slither of gravel that comes from a foot dislodging a patch of scree. I stared all around. '*Co tha'n sud?*' I called, and then, once more: 'Who is there?'

There was no reply, not the least sound. I started forward again – and stopped. Something had moved ahead of me, looming up out of the mist, the size of it that gigantic, it was terrible to behold. I took a quick step back, not able for more, if the truth be told, the strength clean gone from my limbs.

And, then, I started to laugh, for the veil of mist parted, and the spectre that had so frightened me took on the shape of a pony; a chestnut mare with a long silver mane and tail. I laughed – aye, laughed, clown that I was. But the laughing soon stopped when it came to me that I had seen the pony before – that this was the chestnut mare that had stood so patiently beside Miss Fiona only yesterday morning.

I went up to the pony, speaking her name, and she stood still while I patted her long mane, wondering all the time what the beast could be doing on this side of the hill, without her mistress.

The rising wind drove back the swirling mist, and I saw the sheer face of black rock rising high on my right, a sheen of water trickling slowly down its pitted face. I had wandered too far to the north, and would need to work south to reach the pass by the short-cut.

There a was clump of stunted scrub a few yards ahead, growing on the lip of a cut in the ground; a cut that all who knew the hill avoided, for it plunged deep underground. Something white was fluttering in the branches of the scrub. I left the pony and went slowly forward and plucked the satin hair ribbon free. I stuffed it into my pocket. Fearful of what might meet my eyes, I got down on my hands and knees and peered over the lip of the narrow cut in the ground.

It was no more than a yard across at the top, and the half of that hidden by overhanging scrub, but it opened out into a wide chimney of rock, falling sheer for about fifteen feet, when it broadened into a low-roofed cavern about the size of a big room. Miss Fiona was lying on her back at the bottom of the cavern, one leg doubled under her. Blood streaked the white of her forehead. Her eyes were closed.

'Fiona!' I called. 'Fiona''

She never spoke, or moved, never even opened her eyes. I stood up and looked around wildly. Standing there on the mist-wreathed hill-side, not a sound to be heard save the faint murmur of the distant surf, I might have been the only man in the world. Sure enough, I was the only one who knew she was there.

I looked down at her again, lying there with the stillness of death on her. The pony whinnied, as I lowered myself over the edge of the cut, and started to climb down.

Chapter 14

Lachlann Ban once told me that strength of will was more important than strength of body. If only the will was there, he said, and a man had a sense of purpose to which he could direct that will, his body could be made to do wonders.

Those words of Lachlann Ban must have lain dormant in my mind, because I thought I had forgotten them long ago. But they came back to me now, as I tested my holds and cautiously let go of the long branch of scrub that was my only contact with the world above ground. Clinging tightly to the bare rock of the shaft, I started to descend slowly, searching with care for finger and toe-holds, and never moving more than a few inches at a time.

The first five or six feet was easy enough. Seen from above, the rock of the shaft presented a smooth face, but now that I was pressed close against it I could see that it was fissured with tiny cracks, and pimpled with little whorls and knobs, too small to catch the eye from a distance but big enough to enable desperate hands and feet to maintain a hold.

I was about half-way down when I felt the rock suddenly slimy against my toes, and my feet started to slip. I got a fresh purchase, and glanced down, thinking it was sweat that had caused me to lose my grip, but no. There was water oozing out of the cracks in the rock, lichen and moss growing in the crevices. Every hand and foothold had become a treacherous snare for the unwary. From now on, I moved with renewed caution.

It happened with such speed, I was not aware of my feet

slipping from under me. All I knew was that I was suddenly hanging by my fingertips, feet thrashing desperately as I tried to make them stick on a hold. I thought the bones of my fingers must break under the fearful pull of my body weight, but, at last, I managed to get my toes hooked on a ledge. I clung to the face of the rock, panting with relief now that the terrible strain was gone from my fingers. It was sweat that was troubling me now, sweat that covered my hands in a greasy film. I took my left hand away and rubbed it dry on my jersey; got a firm grip again, and let go with my right hand. As I wiped the sweat away, I felt my feet slipping again. I clawed at the rock with my right hand, found my hold, and hung there, my feet scrabbling wildly for a purchase. Again and again, they slipped on the slimy rock. This time, the strain on my fingers was too great to bear. I felt them slowly losing their hold. Slowly – so slowly that I seemed to be watching another person coming to grief – I lost my grip, and fell.

I landed on a patch of wet moss and deep gravel, close to Fiona, not on rock as I had feared. I was bruised and winded, but none the worse for the fall. As I struggled to my feet, I noticed that my hands were skinned and bleeding, and I wondered dully why I felt no hurt.

I bent over Fiona. She had not moved as far as I could see. She was still lying on her back, with her right leg doubled under her, hands spread limply by her side. There was a deep gash across her brow, the dried blood matted in her hair. She was breathing fast, though, and, as I watched, she moved her head a little to one side.

I took off my jersey and made a pillow of it and slipped it under her head. I looked a right tinker seeing the shirt I was wearing was an old one of my father's, split at the elbows, but I was past caring about the like of that.

I looked up at the long shaft that rose out of the roof of the cavern like a tall chimney, and I was sick at heart with fear; a fear that struck home with numbing despair, extinguishing all hope as surely as the meeting of a thumb and forefinger snuffs the flame of a candle. The sloping roof of the underground cave was far higher than I had thought when looking down from the top. Stretching on tiptoe, I was still inches short of the start of the rock chimney. Without the aid of a rope from above, I could never hope to climb up again. Unless someone found us, the cave would be our tomb.

I started shouting for help my voice echoing hollowly around the walls of the cavern. But I soon tired of that. Who would ever hear a faint voice issuing feebly from a narrow cut in the ground at a place in the hill that rarely saw a human being? A wandering shepherd might walk this way – but with the marines expected in the place what shepherd would be roaming the hill today?

I got down on my knees beside the still figure of the girl, desperate for the sound of a voice that was not the mocking echo of my own. 'Fiona!' I said urgently. 'Fiona!'

Her rapid breathing never changed. There was not even the flicker of an eyelid to show that she had heard her name being called.

A little stream trickled across the floor of the cavern. I ripped the sleeve off my shirt where it was torn at the elbow, and dipped it in the water and bathed her face. She moved her head restlessly, and opened her eyes.

'Fiona,' I said, 'are you hurt bad?'

She looked at me blankly, like someone awakening from a deep sleep. Her tongue moved slowly over her lips. Then, awareness lit her eyes, and she smiled at me. 'Alasdair!' she whispered.

It was the very first time she had spoken my name – indeed, until that moment I was not aware that she knew of me by name at all – and such was my glad surprise I forgot for the moment that we were trapped deep underground, if you can believe such a thing.

'What time is it?' she said weakly.

'Morning. Not long after dawn, I reckon.'

'What – what day?'

'What day?' I said, thinking her mind was wandering. 'Tuesday – Tuesday morning.'

'Where am I?'

'Down a hole in the ground. On our side o' the hill. You must have fallen.'

'I remember. Last night. The mist was frightful. Jess stumbled and threw me. I remember blundering into bushes – and then . . .' Her voice tailed off.

'Where were you going?' I said, unable to hold back any longer.

'To find you. Warn you.' She tried to lift her head, and bit her lip to stifle the gasp of pain. 'Quick!' she said faintly. 'You have got to stop them.'

'Is the pain bad?' I said, certain sure now that she was wandering.

'A bit. When I try to move. But you must go. The marines know you are going to block the pass. They have sent gunboats with more troops. If the pass is blocked, they are going to land from the sea and evict all the people from their homes. Sheriff Ivory has given the orders.'

She was panting. The talking had drained every scrap of her strength. But I could not leave it at that.

'How did you know we are going to block the pass?' I said.

'Last night.' She moistened her lips. 'Two men came to see the factor. They told him. I saw them. Heard them.' Her eyelids started to droop. Her voice had sunk to a whisper. It was that low I had to bend over her to catch the words. 'I heard them talking – Sheriff Ivory and Colonel Munro, too. It's true.' She swallowed, and moistened her lips again, her eyes drooping shut. 'If you block the pass,' she murmured, 'the marines will land from the sea . . . evict the people. Sheriff Ivory said it would be . . . an act of . . . rebellion against the Government.'

'The two men,' I said, knowing her strength to be gone, but unable to contain myself. 'Did you see them? Did you see the two men, Fiona?'

She was silent, her eyes fast shut. I went across to the little stream, and soaked the makeshift cloth, my head fairly spinning at the import of her news. Something – some instinct that bore no relation to my thoughts – made me look up the tall chimney of rock at the very moment that a head appeared over the lip of the cut. It was Domhnull the shepherd staring down at me, and it would be hard to say which of us had the biggest surprise. All I can say for certain is that I was the first to find my tongue.

'Get ropes, Domhnull,' I shouted, a feeling of joyous relief sweeping over me. 'Get Lachlann Ban and the rest down from the pass. The laird's daughter is hurt bad.'

He did not waste time on words, Domhnull. He rose to his feet, and was off in an instant, and I saw that he was clutching the reins of Fiona's pony in his fist.

I turned to her, and saw, to my surprise, that her eyes were wide open. 'That man,' she whispered. 'He was the one who brought the news to the factor. Him, and a little man with a stick – a cripple.'

It is bad to be in the grip of despair, knowing yourself to be trapped without hope of relief, but it is a thousand times worse to discover that the friendly face of a rescuer is the treacherous mask of an enemy. If Domhnull the shepherd had played us traitor, he was not going to rush to the pass and return with Lachlann Ban and the rest before the damage had been done, and Sheriff Ivory could land more marines from the sea and evict the people on the excuse that they were in revolt against the Government. And if Fiona had seen himself and Seumas Crubach at the factor's house, was it not likely that they, in turn, had clapped eyes on her. If that was so, Domhnull the shepherd must be wondering how she had come to fall into the underground cavern, and how I came to be along with her. Might he not suspect that she had come to warn me; that we had arranged to meet on the hill, and she had lost her way in the mist? If that suspicion entered his mind, would he ever return with a rescue party? He had taken the chestnut mare away with him. What if he set the pony free on another part of the hill? There was no hope of anyone coming near the entrance to the cavern if the pony was not seen grazing nearby.

I was glad that Fiona's eyes were closed, for I do not know how I could have faced her knowing what I did.

Time and again, I prowled the length and breadth of the cavern, made active by the restless tumult of my thoughts rather than any hope of discovering a means of escape. I must have turned at the far end of the cave a score of times before I noticed that the little stream flowed out of the cave through a narrow slit in the rock. It was a slit no more than eighteen inches high, and less than twice that in breadth. I lay flat on my chest in the stream, and got my head and shoulders into the opening, but it was too dark to see anything. It seemed to be some kind of tunnel in the rock, sloping down from the level of the cavern.

I got to my feet and went back to Fiona. Her eyes were still closed, and her face seemed to have grown even paler. I squatted down beside her, watching the little stream as it flowed across the floor of the cavern and out through the slit in the rock. Did it end in an underground loch, or did it find its way out to the open hill-side again? There was many a place in the hill where a stream gushed out of an opening in the rock. Was this the start of one of them?

I sat there for minutes that had to me the substance of hours before I gained the will to make the decision to find out.

With my arms bent to take the weight off my chest and stomach, it was easy enough wriggling a way into the tunnel. As it sloped downwards, I was able to drag myself along without any great difficulty.

I was sure it was veering to the left, and the third time I cracked my head on the roof I knew for certain that the tunnel was narrowing. The roof was that low my chin was hardly ever out of the icy stream, and I felt my shoulders starting to scrape against the walls. I angled myself on to my left shoulder, and for the next few yards the going was easier.

I laboured on, felt the rock resisting the passage of my right shoulder, and clawed at the bed of the stream, trying to lever myself forward. I slid forward and stopped, a weight of rock seeming to constrict my chest. Gravel moved under my hands. They were too numb to feel hurt when I encountered bare rock, but despite the effort I made my body did not move an inch. I tried to draw up my legs and push with my toes, but the roof of the tunnel was too low to enable me to move sufficiently to gain a proper purchase. I lay still for a while, getting my breath back, tasting the bitter gall of defeat. Well, I had done my best. No man could do more. I would just have to make my way back to the cavern.

I braced my hands on the bed of the stream, and pushed hard. Nothing happened. I tried again. And again. And again.

I was stuck fast in the tunnel, unable to go forward or back!

I do not want to dwell on the terror that gripped me at that moment. It seemed as if the whole tremendous weight of the hill was being borne by my own frail body. It was bearing down on my back and slowly crushing the life out of me. It seemed as if my ribs would crack under the strain; as if tortured lungs must surely burst; that the icy water lapping my chin must rise and drown me. *Dhia*, if I live to be as stricken in years as old Diarmad, and have a beard as white as he, and sit quiet while young men speak of strife, I will never forget the blinding terror of being stuck fast in the bowels of the earth.

A voice within me goaded me on to frantic struggle; a voice like a clarion call compared to the muted whisper that murmured: *Keep calm! Keep calm!* I shut my ear to that furious clamour – how, I know not – and lay still, lay as still as any corpse, close-boxed in its coffin.

Little by little, the terrified leaping of my heart slowed to a steadier beat; the choking pressure on my throat eased, and I was able to breathe again. Breathe, did I say? Draw breath would be nearer the mark. I was able to draw breath after what seemed an age without air.

I tried to move, not forward or back, but from side to side, in a rolling motion. My thin shirt shredded at the shoulders. Heedless of the rock walls tearing my skin, I struggled on – *I was moving!* My left shoulder slid down until my face was under water. I wriggled forward, felt my right shoulder slide free, and plunged clear of the constricting walls of the tunnel.

It must have been a bottleneck that had held me, because the walls widened with every move I made, until I could not feel them with the outstretched span of my arms. I was crawling on my hands and knees now, the water halfway up my forearms. There were clefts in the walls where more hidden streams flowed out to join the main channel, and the noise of rushing water was loud in my ears. There could be no turning back, I knew that well enough, but I tried not to think about what might lie ahead.

Suddenly, without warning, the bed of the stream fell away beneath my hands, and I floundered wildly, out of my depth. There was a roaring in my ears as I broke the surface. I was plucked forward, like a cork in a surging tide, flung against rocky walls in a swift, stormy passage that battered me near insensible before I was spewed out on the open hill-side.

I rolled over and over, coming to a stop against a pillar of rock, dazed and half-drowned, blinking in the sudden light of day, too bemused to realize that I was free. All I could do was lie still, gasping in great lungfuls of air, feeling the drizzle of rain on my face like a blessed kiss of life.

I do not know how long I lay there, staring up at the steep hill-side where a stream gushed out of a cleft in the rock – the stream that had swept me to safety. Minutes, perhaps. I do not know. When you have been near death, the count of time by the measure of the clock has no meaning.

I got to my feet and gazed around in wonder. I was no more than six hundred yards from the cut in the ground that marked the entry to the underground cavern where Fiona was trapped – six hundred yards to the south, and far down the hill.

I looked out to sea. Two gunboats were riding at anchor in the roadstead close offshore, their tall masts standing out sharp against the skyline. I turned again to the hill, and gazed up at the pass. All but the topmost peaks were clear of mist.

A bugle call sounded, sharp and clear, over the hill to the west. Before the last notes had died away, I started to run.

Chapter 15

Let no man tell you that under its thin skin of sparse soil the hill is dead stone, a cold monument of a fierce up-heaval in the days when the world was young. The hill is more than that. The hill is there to fight all who challenge its dominion. It fought me, every terrible foot of the way, as I struggled to gain the heights above the pass, and I was not lacking, I am telling you. I ran as if I could feel the hot breath of Satan himself searing my neck; ran as I had never run before – or ever will again, if the truth be told. The pale image of the printed word can give you no idea of the torture that was in that run, or bring home to you how my puny strength was broken and destroyed entire by the power of the hill.

On and on, I ran, following the narrow sheep track that wound between tumbled rocks and fallen boulders, the age-old droppings of the hill. After the darkness of the underground tunnel, the green of the close-cropped turf was that bright it very near dazzled me.

On and on, climbing all the time, lungs gasping greedily for air, feet sliding across patches of loose scree, as I skirted a great rock buttress, for all the world like the wall of an ancient castle. Up and up, the wind rising all the time as the way grew steeper, working round the shoulder of the hill where the ground was ravaged by the deep scars of winter streams; leaping over a foaming burn, stumbling and falling. Up again, heart pounding madly, staggering forward on legs of straw. Falling. Rising, Falling again.

I had to take a rest. The drizzle was cool on my sweating

face. Far below, I could see the gleaming black faces of the peat bogs; a sheen of silver skirting them where the surface water had gathered in pools. Ahead, the rounded breast of the hill fell in grooved patterns of brown rock and green turf to a cluster of lochans, bright with movement, as the wind rippled their waters.

Up again, and on, forcing weary limbs into a battle they were past enduring. The hill resisting, fighting back every foot of the way. On and on, knees creaking at the joints, thighs and calves aching with fatigue, every beat of my heart a slamming pain in my breast. I stumbled and fell. Lying inert, gasping for breath, I looked down at the long stretch of bog far below. It was veined with tiny streams, and I wondered wildly if it, too, lived and breathed and suffered; if that tracery of veins fed a palpitating heart deep in the bog?

Up once more, feeling an icy bite in the wind, the scree sliding under my bone-weary feet. I went down with the falling scree, and lay spread-eagled on the slope, gazing at the white stones embedded deep in the green hill-side, thinking stupidly they must be the bodies of dead sheep. Dead sheep on a green hill. I repeated the words, aloud. *Dead sheep on a green hill.*

I got to my knees, and crawled clear of the scree. Up again, reeling like a drunk man; a clamorous drumbeat pounding inside my head, until I felt it must burst. Knees bent, hands clawing at the steep hill – climbing, climbing, for ever climbing! Stumbling and falling; staggering on my feet the one minute – crawling on my hands and knees the next.

There was no longer smooth turf underfoot. Now, it was all rock and scree. The jagged peaks loomed up out of the swirling mist, like giant sentinels doomed to keep eternal watch. I clung to a boulder, sobbing and retching. A great spread of coastline lay below stretching out to the south. I could see as far as the jutting finger of Rudha nam

Braithrean. It was like being suspended from a cloud. I looked away, turned dizzy by the sight of that great expanse of land far below.

On again, unable to believe that I had climbed so high. One . . . two . . . three uncertain steps forward, and I was down. I tried to get on my knees, but my strength was spent. My body seemed to be drifting apart; my head a fiery balloon floating free of the rest of me, glad to shed the spent and useless flesh.

I heard the swift rush of feet, right enough, although I was too far gone to open my eyes. Strong arms supported me. I was aware of them carrying me; laying me down gently. A bottle was pressed to my lips. I started to cough. *Dhia*, how I coughed! The raw whisky was burning my throat, lighting a fire in my belly. I opened my eyes, and saw the familiar faces all around, saw them through a swimming haze. I blinked it away, wondering why they were all gazing at me as if I had grown two heads.

I looked beyond them to the mighty array of boulders, piled high, ready for casting down on the pass below. A wild laugh bubbled in my throat. I choked it down; hid it in another fit of coughing.

They heard me in silence, as I gasped out my story, every eye intent on my face. And when I was done those eyes turned as one to gaze at Lachlann Ban, waiting on him for the first word.

He looked away from them, staring moodily at the massed boulders, and down at the narrow walls of the pass. He turned slowly, and gazed out to sea at the gunboats lying offshore, and his face was as bleak as the harsh crags all around. When he spoke, he did not look at any of them, and that was not like him. Indeed, it was almost as if he was talking to himself.

'It was not the marines got the better of us,' he said, 'it was our own people. Good grief, I never thought I would see the day when men of our own kind would hand a knife to

Sheriff Ivory and give that rag of a man the chance to plunge it deep in our backs.'

Colla the smith was always slow on the uptake. Trust him to say, 'What are we to do, Lachlann?'

'Do?' Lachlann Ban demanded, looking at the smith with eyes that fairly glittered. He threw back his head and laughed – and, my word, it was some laugh he made, I am telling you; a laugh that was more like a cry of pain, if my ears played me true. 'We do nothing, *'ille*. We rest our bones, after the stamp of old men that stricken wi' years they would count it a victory to live the long night through and glimpse the light o' day again. Only it is not the day we are waiting to see, but the going o' the marines – supposing they make off once they have marched through the land and found none to oppose them. And we are not stricken in years – it is treachery that has laid us low.' He clenched his fists, and brought them down on his thighs, as if the heads of Domhnull the shepherd and Seumas Crubach were there to meet the blows. '*Dhia*, I could choke on such words, but what else is there for it? What way can we stand and face them like men wi' another crowd o' marines lying offshore, and Sheriff Ivory ready to slip the leash from them, and give the word to unroof every homestead in the place, supposing we block the pass?'

He looked at them all in turn. Nobody spoke.

It was my father who broke the silence at last. 'Aye, we must let them through,' he said slowly, 'that is all about it.'

Lachlann Ban – Ian Beag and Eachunn Ruadh along with him – had gone to rescue Fiona from the underground cavern. The rest of us watched the coming of the marines from the secret green place high to the north of the pass. There was only a wisp of mist on the crags, poised like a long, grey pennant, as the advance guard came into view.

They were led by a helmeted officer, wearing a long sword, twenty men at his back, marching in double file, their muskets slung on their shoulders. The officer brought them to a halt before they reached the pass, and the leading four marines were dispatched as scouts, running awkwardly, in their long greatcoats, to take up positions on the ridge of the hill where they could command a view of the ground below. The officer drew his sword, and the bugle sounded the march. The advance guard moved on to the pass, the marching feet of the men striking a rhythmic tattoo as they vanished into the rocky defile.

The rain was falling heavily as the main body of the marines drew near. The long, long column of marching men kept blurring before my eyes, so it was in me to believe that I was seeing them through a fog of sleep, and would waken presently to find little Seoras warm beside me, and know I was safe in bed at home.

It was like a bad dream, right enough, seeing that great column of marching men, the officers mounted on ponies, streaming through the pass and pouring down the winding road to the plain far below. And at their back came a coach and four – my father whispering, 'Sheriff Ivory, for sure!' as it went by – and behind the coach came two wagonettes, crowded with men in civilian clothes, and a squad of police on foot.

Bugle calls sounded as the long column neared the croft lands, their challenging notes reaching us high in the hills, but not a man appeared to do battle. The marines might have been marching through a desert, for there was not a living person to be seen. Every man in the place would be peering out at them from behind barred doors – Tomas the Elder down on his knees, I would not wonder.

The clouds were hanging low over the sea, the tall masts of the gunboats faintly visible through the driving rain, as the armed column streamed across the plain, and headed for the road to the shore. I laid my burning face against the cold, wet rock and closed my eyes, the tramp of marching feet still resounding in my head.

I heard my father say, 'They must be going to embark seeing they are making for the shore. Well, well, it takes two to make a fight, right enough, but who would have the wisdom to turn the other cheek supposing he thought he had the least chance o' winning?'

Colla the smith snorted, 'The laird will have his way of it from this day on. You will never get anyone in the place to stand against the laird now they have clapped eyes on the power he has at his back.'

I got to my feet, saying peevishly, 'Wait you till Fiona tells him what has been going on in this place. It will be changed days once Fiona tells him what she knows.'

They were gaping at me, every one of them, and a sudden anger seized me; a rage so great that I felt myself trembling. But that was a piece of foolishness. They would be wondering who Fiona was, for not one of them knew her by name.

I started to laugh; laughed so hard that the ground tilted under me. I mind Colla the smith starting forward, his arms spread wide. Colla caught me as I fell, and I knew no more.

Chapter 16

I discovered, long afterwards, that they all thought I was going to die, like many a one before me in this place who had got rheumatic fever bad. But it was different for me. I did not have to fight an unequal struggle for life, penned in a corner of a small, crowded room, with the mistress of the house trying to make every shilling that came her way do the work of two, and little enough to spare for food, let alone medicines. It was the laird who saved me. He had me rushed to Inverness, and sent on to a big hospital in Glasgow.

Fiona was the lucky one. She had no bones broken, and the knock on her head was not serious. Indeed, she had fully recovered when I was still deep in the fever, hovering between life and death, sweating out a long nightmare from which it seemed there was to be no awakening. Even when the fever ebbed, and they told me I was doing fine, it was all like a dream, lying there in a hospital bed in the heart of a great city I had never clapped eyes on, being attended by nurses, as if I belonged to the ranks of the gentry.

It was during those lonely months in hospital, chained to a bed for the first time in my life, that I was able to piece together the full story of the treachery of Domhnull the shepherd and Seumas Crubach, and understand the part the factor had played in our troubles. Some of it I heard from Fiona, who came to see me with her father, and some I gleaned from the *Maighstir's* letters – one every week: he was faithful at the letter-writing, I will say that for him – and some I thought out for myself.

The factor was at the root of our troubles. He had been working behind the laird's back, taking advantage of his absence to increase the rents and make life difficult for us in every way he could, in the hope that we would rebel. He was wanting an excuse to clear us from our crofts, so that all our land could be added to the tacksman's sheep farm. Seeing that the tacksman was a relation of his, there was no doubt the scheme would have profited him. Domhnull the shepherd was the creature who kept him supplied with information, and Domhnull got his news from Seumas Crubach, whose spiteful tongue was not slow in blackening the rest of us. Domhnull's reward was to be land of his own, once we were cleared from the place.

The night after I was taken ill the laird had the three of them brought before him. Domhnull the shepherd swore that the factor had promised him land if he would keep him posted with news of any lawless talk, and he made out that the factor had dropped hints of the sort of things he would like to hear – talk that the land belonged to the people, not the laird; news of the blacksmith making weapons; threats of violence – and he claimed that all he did was pass on the news that Seumas Crubach gave him.

The laird wanted to know why Domhnull did not fetch help right away when he found Fiona and me in the underground cavern. That made him squirm, I am telling you. It seems that the sweat came out on him that bad you would have thought he was roasting on a spit over the fire instead of fidgeting before the laird's cold gaze. He tried to get out of it by saying that he had taken fright on seeing the marines coming; that he had hidden until they had embarked on the gunboats, and when he went back to the cavern with ropes we had vanished.

The factor denied every word that had been said against him, denouncing Domhnull the shepherd for a rogue and a liar, and accusing him of stealing the tacksman's sheep. It was Seumas Crubach who put a stop to that talk, declaring boldly that the pair of them had got him to write the letter threatening murder to the laird, and it was the factor himself who had said that this was the very thing that would enable Sheriff Ivory to call in the marines and evict us from the land.

Fiona said she was made to leave the room after that, but she listened at the door and heard her father flay them with his tongue something terrible; and, my word, the factor must have taken it bad, to be lashed along with a common shepherd and a crippled tailor, for he was a proud man, who prized his rank above all things.

The three of them were put aboard the mail steamer, *Lochiel*, that very night, and they left the island the next morning. They went willingly, you may be sure, for they were wise enough to know what would have happened to them if they had stayed within reach of the vengeance of the people. I never heard what became of the factor, but there was word that Domhnull had taken ship to Australia. Some said that Seumas Crubach had gone with him, although there were others who claimed that the same one had been seen in Glasgow. And only the other day, a cattle drover, on his way through our township, was telling of a travelling tailor he had met in wild Glen More; a little crippled fellow, with a voice on him fit for a man twice his stature, and a temper as sharp as the needles he carried in his pack. There was only one man to fit that description, so I think Seumas Crubach must be wandering the lonely glens of the mainland.

He was the one who puzzled me, Seumas Crubach. It was easy enough to understand the factor and Domhnull the shepherd – they were acting for gain, and there is never a shortage of men prepared to enrich themselves by turning a blind eye to the law and justice. But it could not have profited Seumas Crubach to have us all evicted, and it came to me, through time, that we were all responsible, in part, for his actions. The guilt was not his alone; every one of us had a share in it.

On Hallowe'en nights, we used to torment him something terrible. I mind one Hallowe'en when a crowd of us boys caught him outside. We were all carrying lanterns, our faces blackened so that he could not tell who was before him, and I can mind to this day the look of terror on his face as we formed a ring round him. He struck out wildly with his stick, and someone snatched it from him. Another gave him a push, and he fell on his back, unable to rise without the aid of his stick. We danced around him, screeching and howling, slapping his face with cabbage leaves, as he lay helpless on his back. I mind how Tomas the Elder's son – aye, the son of Tomas the Elder! – poked poor Seumas Crubach with the stick that had been torn from his grasp, mocking him for a crab, and asking why he was not under a rock on the shore, where he belonged. I mind the tailor, near demented with rage and fear, screaming at us: *'Dhia*, you will pay for this! Supposing it takes me years, you will pay, the whole crowd o' you!' And every Hallowe'en thereafter, he barred the door of his house and boarded the windows, and would not put his nose outside, even when we hurled stones at the door.

Thinking back on it all, it was no wonder to me that his spite made him want to destroy us, even supposing it did not profit him a farthing. But the rest of them in the place were bitter about Seumas Crubach. It was not in them to see that he had just cause for spite, poor man, and those who condemned him the most were the very ones who should have been busy examining their own consciences.

The long winter turned to spring, and spring to early summer before I got clear of the hospital. During my last week there, at the beginning of May, the laird came by himself, and had a long talk with me. The doctors had told him that my heart had been affected by the fever, and

I would never be able to do heavy work, so he was wanting me to take up my schooling again. The *Maighstir* would coach me during the summer months, and the laird planned to send me to a school in Edinburgh in the autumn.

He must have seen the dismay in my eyes, because he said quickly, 'You are not going to be an invalid, Alasdair, but you will have to take care for a long time to come. I know you don't like the idea of being chained to a desk, but the time will pass much quicker than you think, if you apply yourself diligently to your books.'

He smiled at me, and I thought of the day I had faced him for the first time, my legs trembling and my mouth dry with fear. But that had been another life altogether, and I could look back now on the boy who had trembled before the laird and smile myself at the thought of that poor, dead ghost.

'I don't intend to keep you indoors all the time, you know,' he went on. 'Estate management gets a man out in the open. Try not to forget that, boy.'

I was wise enough to know that I was lucky to get the chance of further schooling, and grateful to the laird for the advancement he was offering me. But I could not help counting the cost, and brooding on the way I had made light of my health and strength – taking it as no more than my natural due – in the days when I had the full freedom of my legs, and could do what I pleased in the way of work and play. It was a long time before I saw that every gain in life conceals a loss, and the most a man can hope to do is to stand erect no matter what befalls.

It was the middle of May when I left the hospital, and the laird named the Saturday after my arrival home as the day on which he would announce the details of the reforms he was going to introduce. Mind you, word had leaked out about them already – the tacksman's land to be divided into new crofts; a fair rent to be fixed on the existing crofts;

security of tenure for every one of us – and the place was in a fever of excitement. I believe I was the only one who felt flat, and I wondered why.

It may have been that the long journey home had tired me more than I knew, or perhaps it was the way my mother treated me. There was no scolding from her now; not so much as a single cheep of complaint. She fussed about me all day long, barking at Seoras if he so much as came near me when I had my nose in a book – she, who had always made out that the only book a man was needing was the Bible. But I could do no wrong now – and all because the laird looked well upon me. That was what I hated most, herself measuring my value by the esteem of people she thought above her. That, and the way I sometimes caught my father looking at me – as if he had found a stranger warming himself at his hearth, and was puzzled to know who he was.

All that week, I waited for Lachlann Ban to call at the house, but he never came near. It was not until the Saturday that I saw him. I was standing on the fringe of the great crowd that had gathered in front of the school to await the coming of the laird – the menfolk in their Sabbath clothes, the *cailleachs* in decent black, their bonnets edged with white, and the young girls in dresses of brightly striped homespun drugget – when a hand squeezed my shoulder. I spun round, and he was standing there, the long scar still clearly marking the brown of his face. It was good to grip him by the hand again; no need for words at the feel of that strong clasp.

'You got thin,' he said. And then: 'They tell me you are away to Edinburgh at the end o' the summer.'

I nodded.

'Well, you have got the brains, boy. See and use them. And don't be forgetting the Gaelic just because you are after getting a right education.'

'No fear,' I said.

He looked up at the hill. A coach was coming down the road from the pass; a long line of carriages behind it.

'The laird,' he said. 'And a right parade at his back.' He gave a quick shrug. 'I am away myself, boy. Next month. Bound for Boston.'

'You are not away to America!' I exclaimed.

'Aye.'

'But why, Lachlann?' I demanded. 'We have got what we wanted, haven't we? More land. A fair rent. Security.'

'So they say.'

'Well, it is right enough. That is what the laird is coming to tell them.'

'Aye, the laird,' he said, a flicker of a smile twitching at his lips. 'The laird is coming to tell them, right enough. There is one thing sure, boy, we have still got the laird.'

'Well?'

'Oh, he is a good enough man, it seems, although he neglected the place something terrible in the days when the factor was king. But supposing he gets rid o' the place – makes it over to another laird, in return for a bundle o' money – and ourselves sold along wi' the estate, like dumb cattle beasts being handed over to a new master? How do you know the new laird will treat us fair, eh?' He rubbed at the scar on his cheek, and I waited for him to go on, knowing fine he was not wanting an answer from me. 'Ach, if only they had all stood fast,' he said, at length, 'we could ha' been done wi' the like o' lairds, and worked our ground as free men.'

The *Maighstir* was out at the front of the crowd, glancing at a sheet of paper in his fist. That would be the notes of his speech, for sure. He would be in his glory laying off his chest to them all, with the laird listening. He stuffed the paper into his pocket, and craned his neck, staring over the heads of the crowd. Likely, he would be looking for me. Well, he need not think that I was going out in the front along with him, to have them all gape at me. I saw his sister stop fiddling at her new bonnet, and give his sleeve a tug. The *Maighstir* turned round, and shook hands with the minister.

'Changed days,' Lachlann Ban said, 'to see the minister and the *Maighstir* at the head o' the crowd. I never saw a sight of either o' them when we were in need o' help.'

'Lachlann,' I said, 'why are you making off to America?'

He laid a hand on my shoulder. 'You mind that night we met you above the pass – the night you were on your way back from the factor?'

'Aye, fine.'

'*Dhia*, I have never forgotten that night,' he said. 'When I was coming through the pass, I looked back. Every man was carrying a lighted peat. A poor enough light, a single peat – a pale glimmer just, hardly enough to guide the steps of a man in the dark. But there were that many of them, it looked like a long ribbon o' fire mounting the pass, and I thought, then, see the strength o' them, if only they stand together as free men. But they did not stand boy. When it came to the bit, they melted away in the dark.'

The laird's coach was moving along the road to the bridge, the jet-black ponies stepping proudly. The laird's coach was followed by carriages and gigs and dog carts, the crowded mail coach trailing along at the end of the procession.

'Aye, but how can you change things by going to America?' I demanded.

'It is easier to make a start there,' he said. 'Everything is new. They are not afraid o' change, the way they are here. People are making for America from all over, and for why? Because they cannot get justice in the old world. Every one of them, in his way, is carrying his lighted peat.' He squeezed my shoulder hard, and there was something of the old fierce pride in his voice when he said, 'I am telling

168

you, boy, when we all come together in America, we will light a ribbon o' fire that will circle the earth before it is done.'

He was right enough, in a way, Lachlann Ban; I was not so stupid that I could not see it made sense for him. But not for me. I gazed down at my boots, wondering how I could put into words what I wanted to say to him.

Someone shouted, 'Away for the laird's coach!' and a full score of men, followed by a trail of shouting boys, ran to the bridge and stopped his coach. The coachman got down – a new coachman; Fiona had seen to it that Scobie no longer had the charge of the laird's carriages – and the men unharnessed the ponies, and took over the shafts themselves.

A great cheer rang out as the laird stepped out of the coach in front of the school. He handed down Fiona, and the minister and the *Maighstir* went forward to greet them. They all mounted the decorated cart that was to serve as a platform.

I turned to Lachlann Ban, but he was gone – striding, quick-footed for the open moor. I gazed after him, willing him to look back, but he never once turned his head.

Another cheer rang out – and then a name; a name that was taken up by everyone there. 'Alasdair! Alasdair! Alasdair, ' the crowd chanted.

I wheeled round. The sight of them all facing my way, their backs to the group on the platform, unmanned me, and I was of a mind to make off after Lachlann Ban. Before I could move, I was seized by Colla the smith and Eachunn Ruadh. They hoisted me shoulder-high. I was carried through the cheering crowd and put down on the platform beside Fiona and the laird.

The *Maighstir* took the sheet of paper out of his pocket, and gave a nervous cough. The laird offered me a quick smile, and whispered, 'We had to get you, Alasdair. You belong here.'

I nodded, not feeling ill at ease any more, smiling back at all the eager faces in the crowd that smiled up at me. But I never heard a word of the *Maighstir*'s speech, I was too busy marvelling at the thought that it was from the laird I had been given my answer to Lachlann Ban.

If you liked this story then why not look out for other Kelpies. There are dozens of stories to choose from : ghosts, spy stories, animals and the countryside, witches, mysteries and secrets, adventures and many more. Kelpie paperbacks are available from all good bookshops.

For your free Kelpie badge and complete catalogue please send a stamped addressed envelope to:
Margaret Ritchie (K.C.B.),
Canongate Publishing Ltd.,
17 Jeffrey Street, Edinburgh
EH1 1DR.